I0779451

FLIGHT OF THE STARLING

BOOK ONE
JUSTINE

Christine Merser

Apricity Publishing ✦ Wiscasset, ME 2025

*"At first we will only skim the surface of
the earth like young starlings, but soon,
emboldened by practice and experience,
we will spring into the air with the
impetuousness of the eagle, diverting
ourselves by watching the childish
behavior of the little men or awling
miserably around on the earth below us."*

– Jean-Jacques Rousseau

TABLE OF CONTENTS

PROLOGUE

I sit in the black Prius in an empty parking lot about a mile from the cemetery. The car is in someone else's name. I wear long pants, a long-sleeved shirt and shoes with a flat, unrecognizable sole, one size smaller than my normal shoe size.

No jewelry. Hair hidden, tucked up into a baseball cap without any logo, dyed blonde just for the day. Sunglasses from Walmart.

I patiently wait for the text telling me it's safe to drive to the gravesite. Coming here is not only risky, but a gluttonous waste of money. I don't care.

Ping.

The book arrived. Thanks for sending.

It's code for the area has been swept on foot

and a drone is overhead making sure there are no eyes in the air or approaching. The cemetery's cameras are interrupted for the next fifteen minutes. I'm free to drive to the grave.

I put the car in drive and head to the entrance. Earlier I had memorized exactly where to go as if I'd been here before.

I pull up on the side of the winding road where I can walk the few steps to the grave, and immediately notice a majestic tree that has to be at least a hundred years old. I spot the marker beneath and wonder how they were able to secure such a seasoned space for a burial that's only a few months old. Was someone else moved?

I take a deep breath and put forth thoughts of grateful appreciation that the woman buried here has such a quiet place to rest. Keeping my emotions in check, I try to focus on what I came here to say.

I get out of the car and walk purposefully to the marker. I use short, quick steps, not my normal gait. I rub my shoulder as I walk. It still bothers me, or maybe I should say I'm always aware of it. The gunshot wound has healed but is an ever-present reminder of it all.

I look down at the simple lettering on the marker. Just her name and dates of birth and death.

Nothing else. What else is there to say? I pause for a moment, head down, and think about the first time I met her. How so much has changed. How *I've* changed. I think about how it could have been me in the ground here.

I know not to speak out loud, so I say what I came to say to myself. "I'm not even sure why I'm here. I still wonder at your motivation. Was the story you told me true? Was the connection of our last meeting real? It felt real at the time.

"I'm pretty sure I wouldn't be here without you. I came to tell you that. You will be with me every waking moment for the rest of my life. Lives were changed.

"I thank you for helping me. I won't be back, but I will remember you. If things had been different for both of us, we might have been friends."

Then I turn, walk back to the car exactly the way I came, and drive away. The entire visit takes less than three minutes.

The drone hovers over the cemetery for another hour and then heads south.

CHAPTER ONE

The Man

His estate is on the ocean, surrounded by those vibrant green hedges that magazines are named after. Perfectly trimmed with precision hospital corners. Palm trees dot the sky above the hedges, swaying in the breeze. The entrances all look the same.

Palm Beach in the winter. Hamptons in the summer. The only difference is the kind of trees behind the hedges. The people? They're the same. Finance titans, political power brokers, artists, celebrities, old money. They all covet an invite to the lunches and dinners hosted on the property daily.

The man in residence is more than respected in financial circles. Being at his home, in this setting, with conversations around politics, culture, sports and current events, is where those in the know want to be.

The man who calls this hedge-hidden fortress his winter home is Robert Bradbury, and he's worth billions. No one knows for sure exactly how many.

Robert is in his seventies with an amazing athleticism that includes helicopter drop skiing and tennis doubles with three pros. The pros don't coddle him. They're told to challenge him with a back-and-forth that isn't an easy win.

He likes to win, and that *is* the point, but he isn't afraid of losing. That's what sets him apart. At one point he told me that "people try to take a loss and stick with it until it becomes a win. I don't do that. I let go of the loss as soon as I realize that's what it is, and then I move on. I win more than I lose. I think that's why." He cares about *how* he plays, which says a lot about how he approaches all things.

And he likes to play backgammon, which has been the backdrop for our connection over the past twenty years. He plays backgammon with me whenever I show up to dine or when we travel with our sons on vacation. I'm a good backgammon player; not world class but rarely less proficient than those at fancy dinner parties and summer soirees.

Robert was born in Ohio, where he never fit in, and knew that he would join Wall Street before he even knew there was a Wall Street. Like Warren Buffet, he loves making money and figuring out how to do it. Unlike Warren, he doesn't hold annual shareholder meetings where he passes around See's Candies and presses the flesh with investors.

He isn't interested in people as much as he's interested in his own thoughts and projects. He has no desire to be in the news about finance, or anything else, for that matter. He's the poster child for not showcasing your own success.

He's never had investors so it's hard to accurately track his success or his investments. He tends to comment on things as he sees them, and when those around him are making mistakes and he is taking advantage of them, he's not quiet about it. He points them out, not in a conquering "I beat you" way, but rather a "not sure why this wasn't apparent to you" way. He foresaw the fall of the Internet stocks in 2000, and right after the stocks fell, bought back all he sold before the crash at an astounding profit.

He also has secrets. I know some of them.

CHAPTER TWO

Backgammon to Black Ops

I pull up to the gate and wave to Douglas
who is at the entrance. He lets me right in. He has
been part of the staff for years, and he knows me
and I always ask about his family and his health.
I like familiarity around routines that pairs with
longevity. I like that some things don't change in
this world. It's comforting.

My ex-husband, or H1 as I like to refer to
him, and I go way back with Robert and his now
ex-wife, Beth. After my divorce, brought about by
me and the realization that I just couldn't call this
the life I wanted anymore, I steered clear of most of
those who came to me through our marriage. But
the Bradburys were different.

Beth is my best friend, and our kids are tied at the hip. Although Robert and Beth are now divorced, I still spend time with both of them. Beth does the same with H1. We both know it's good for the kids, who might be overlooked by the enormity of the lives of the men we once called husbands.

As I walk through the door on this sunny afternoon, I think, "What am I even doing here?"

But I know why I'm here. I like that he always wants me to sit next to him, when everyone else wants to be sitting next to him. And that at the end of the lunch, when the guests are watching for even a small opening to get their five minutes with him, he always steers me to the backgammon table. They are left standing disappointed, and I like that they admire my stature with him. I guess you might call this an ego-driven relationship, but underneath there's more. A comfort level maybe. I'm not sure.

When others comment on the attention he affords me, I look confused. Just another one of the techniques a person raised to be a chameleon has in their arsenal; choosing how you respond for the effect it will have, as opposed to your true reaction. I've come to realize that my upbringing was all about the appearance of things; how they seemed to others, rather than the truth of my family's needs or beliefs.

I step out of my car and head to the yard where lunch will be served promptly at 1 p.m. It's hot and I marvel at the fact that for some reason there always seems to be a breeze in rich people's back yards no matter what the temperature.

He's not there yet. His day is planned like a chocolate soufflé, with no room for error. His 10:30 a.m. tennis game is always an hour and a half. His shower and fifteen minutes of financial market phone calls end at 12:59 p.m., when he will then walk out to the assembled crowd of guests, go through the buffet and sit down for lunch.

I walk into the crowd of guests. I don't stand out, but one-on-one, I can be mesmerizing. I quickly ascertain what matters to the person with whom I'm paired, and I then become someone who makes them feel fabulous. Brilliant, if brilliance matters. Beautiful, if beauty matters. Funny, if humor matters.

I've been told I'm attractive, or I should say cute. Athletic cute. More pounds than a trophy wife but the kind of athletic body that moves well. Thick brown hair. Strong legs. Girl next door. Prom queen. Classic dresser. Valentino works well.

I walk over to William Reid, the family lawyer and another person who has been around for years.

"William, how was your trip to South America? Is it as bad as they say it is?" I had heard he was on a mission to bring legal help to third world South American countries whose leaders didn't like the law unless they had written it.

"Justine," he bestows the perfunctory kiss. "I have to tell you it was eye-opening to be sure. I forgot about …"

At that moment Robert arrives and everyone notices without acknowledgement. He beelines over to our group and says, "Justine, sit with me. I have some things to discuss." He and I head over to the buffet, and we sit down and others scramble to fill the empty seats.

It used to be more fun. Beth and I always sat together filling our table with who we considered the most interesting people there. We laughed a lot. Irreverent we were. Conversations about men's fascination with pencil sharpeners might take place. Or the news on the next Met Gala's theme and who they were trying to get to chair it. And there would always be a plate of Ring Dings and Ho Hos set down just for our table because Beth and I used to be able to eat them with guilt-free abandon.

One day years before, a French banker was at our table and he looked at the plate of Ring Dings and asked, "What are those?"

Beth, without missing a beat said, "It's the American version of your chocolate macaron. Try one."

He did and loved it. We somehow felt vindicated that this French connoisseur was savoring the plastic wrapped lunchbox treat with a longer-than-lifespan shelf life.

Robert ignores those around us and asks me if I've read the latest article about how the still shocking and new Rainer White House is giving the Middle East priority status that their human rights abuses shouldn't warrant. His indiscretion in sharing classified information is throwing all things FBI and CIA into turmoil.

I had and say so.

He continues, "What's interesting is that things we would never have done, or even known about are now part of a policy to support those who will serve our President with favors and compliments; because the frightening leader of the free world loves pomp and circumstance dedicated to his greatness, and wealth added to his personal coffers."

He spends the rest of the lunch filling me in on what's happening in the year-old administration and what he thinks it means. Others listen, but he ignores them. They try to interject a unique point of view to be interesting. They aren't. When you're more concerned about impressing someone who is never impressed than actually speaking your authentic opinion, you will never be interesting.

He's finished in forty-five minutes, and he gets up and motions me over to a side table at the other end of the patio. Underneath a wonderful shade tree, the backgammon board is already set up. I wasn't finished with lunch, so I pick up my glass of Diet Coke and a ginger molasses cookie from the plate at the center of the table and walk behind him to the board.

We start to play. A few wander over to watch, but once they realize that's all they can do, that no conversation will take place, they leave quietly. Eventually, it's just the two of us, the dice, and the doubling cube.

He owes me thousands of dollars and has never paid me a dime. I also suspect he never thinks I'm a better player than him either, regardless of the running score which he keeps in his head accurately.

I had decided years earlier that the goal for me was that he would one day say, "Justine, you are a better player than me, and I admire that."

Robert most likely never thinks about giving that kind of compliment. Nor does he need one himself. He doesn't care. He just wants to play, and while he sometimes asks me why I've made a move, generally I don't think he notices me or my place at the table. Perhaps I'm just a bit player in his routine of mental and physical stimulation.

I've been playing competitive backgammon since I was nineteen years old. My father made a deal with the Father of Backgammon in America, Prince Alexis Obolensky, to teach me in return for free rooms at the hotel my father owned in the Caribbean where "Obie" held world tournaments in the seventies. Obie was a hustler. So was my father.

Robert finishes his move, looks up at me and says, "I need you to go somewhere for me."

"Where?"

He stops. He puts the cup with his dice down on the board and looks up at me. I meet his gaze, confused. He takes a deep breath and says, "Justine, I need you to go to the Middle East."

He pauses, "You have to take over for a now in-custody woman who has provided trafficked girls to obscenely wealthy men over there for years. I have a team of ex-CIA, Middle Eastern specialists, and ex-FBI agents who have put a plan together.

I need you to go in and help execute that plan. It must be done right away."

He takes another breath. "The woman was taken into custody and if we don't move now, the doorway in will close. Once they suspect she's compromised, they will close it all down and we lose our opportunity. I want you to come here tomorrow morning and meet with the men working on this and then hopefully leave in the next few days."

I look at him, stunned. I wait for him to elaborate. He doesn't. He just picks up his dice and waits for me to make a move. So, I pick up the cube, turn it to two and push it over to him. "I double you." It's all I can think to say.

He accepts.

Five minutes of rolling dice and moving checkers ensue before I speak again.

I finally stop, raise the cup with my dice in it, and look at him until he looks up. I can't read anything in his eyes. Nothing.

"Wait." I pause. "Let me understand this. You want me to go to the Middle East and pretend to be a woman who, in reality is in federal custody, to meet with what I assume are very dangerous men about trafficked girls?"

"Yes."

I say nothing. H1, who is an M&A investment banker, taught me that sometimes the best tactic in a negotiation is silence. "It disarms them," he'd said, "and you will have the upper hand. No one likes silence. They will fill it with words that don't serve them well."

I wait and realize that the theory works for most, but not necessarily someone like Robert. But I refuse to roll the dice and I wait it out.

Finally, Robert continues, "Don't get ahead of it. Just come tomorrow morning and we will walk you through it. We'll then assess what happens next after we see how the trip goes.

"All the work I have done, many have done, rides on keeping channels open there. That is the goal, and you will be the gatekeeper. The woman we have been watching for two years was taken into custody a few days ago. We have to move up our operation, or it will all have been for nothing."

Why is he doing this? Operation? What do you mean *operation*? I don't know anyone who does operations except for doctors. Channels to what? Gatekeeper? I don't say anything out loud. I think to myself that I always say something, but not this time. Finally, I roll the dice, without a word of response, and keep playing until the game is over and we are setting up the next one.

"Robert, this sounds kind of dangerous."

"It's important. You can do it. We will go over it tomorrow."

I have often told people if I had my life to do over again, I would be an FBI agent, like Clarice Starling from *The Silence of the Lambs*, my favorite feminist film of all time. Easy to say when there's no way in hell I would be hired. It's like saying you wished you'd joined the Peace Corps after college, which is always a lie because who wants to sign on for two years somewhere you have no choice in picking and maybe get some worm or parasite that will grow inside you like in that episode of *Grey's Anatomy*? Not someone like me. That's for sure.

Back to *The Silence of the Lambs*. I love Clarice Starling. I love how she faces fear. I love how she keeps her own counsel. I love how she "speaks softly crying to be heard," which is the reference an old friend, David, always quotes when he knows I'm being my naturally strident, over-sharing self.

I have a large poster of Jodie Foster, holding a lamb in my office. I see it every morning and it reminds me that I have a gentle lamb inside of me that I need to take care of, and that I have the strength of Clarice as well. I suspect I don't actually have those traits, but manifesting what you *hope* to be is the new orange from the old black.

So, I look at the poster every morning and try and believe. But let's face it. That poster is safely on the wall in my house, not in my real life. In that moment, I realize I don't have Clarice's strength at all. Nope. Not one bit.

I saw an interview once with Jodie Foster about her role as Clarice. The studio didn't want her to play the part. They wanted a Michele Pfeiffer-type, someone feminine. Pretty. Non-threatening? She went after the role with a certainty that has never been part of my fiber. She told Jonathan Demme, the director, that she loved Starling because she was fighting for all women, and she was fighting all men to save the women. And that not all the men were evil, they were just, well, they were just men. It strikes me that the meeting in the morning will most likely be all men too. In fact, I would bet on it.

My realization that it was the way it had always been, rather than men wanting to keep women beneath them, made it easier for me to believe that change could take place. That men weren't the enemy or even possibly aware of the differences between us.

But I also realize that there *are* bad men who want to keep strong women down. They see the danger in losing their power if women succeed. I know, as I recall this philosophy, that the men Robert is talking about me going to see in the Middle East are the latter. For sure the latter.

We keep playing, Robert saying nothing more and me losing three games in a row. I have no desire to concentrate on the odds around dice and moves when I'm weighing that the odds of me succeeding at some covert operation like this are not necessarily in my favor.

I get up to go to the restroom. I throw water on my face, look in the mirror and I don't see Clarice Starling. I see a fifty-something woman with scared eyes and plain gold earrings who has no idea about real fear or the Middle East. It's a place I've never been to, or wanted to go to, actually, and I have happily traveled the world.

I walk back to the table, sit down, and we each roll the dice for the opening move. It's 3-1, the perfect opening roll securing someone's 5-point position, but it's his. I pick up the dice and look at him across the table. Again, he looks up, surprised, and meets my gaze.

"Robert, I'm a photographer. I take pictures of people. Portraits. I sit on a bunch of boards. I'm a mom. Tennis player. Backgammon player. You know what I'm not? I'm not a spy. I assume this is not a surprise to you.

"Why are you picking me for this and what makes you think I can do it? I can't lie to my son about what I had for dinner last night, or the pint of ice cream afterward. How am I going to go and do this?"

He puts the cup with his dice in it on the board, sits back in his chair and says nothing for a long moment. He just looks at me. He doesn't look away, but I can tell he is going to choose his words carefully.

"All my life, I've done everything aboveboard. And I have paid dearly for it. We have known each other a long time. I trust you. Doing what needs to be done has to be done by someone from my inner circle who I trust. That person can't be known publicly. That person needs to be smart and calm, and we both know you are both those things.

"You don't care about my wealth, or my fame, or any of that. My team has evaluated you for the last few months. We knew we would need someone.

We did not think it would be this soon. I wanted it to be someone I knew. The rest of the team wanted a seasoned pro from the CIA black ops group.

"Yes, there is a risk factor because we have no idea how you will perform under this kind of pressure, which is different from other kinds of pressure. It means thinking on your feet. It means not showing what you truly think, and you have sat with me at many dinners where I had no idea what you thought until we spoke of it later. It means playing a role convincingly, and I believe you do that every day of your life.

"The people who looked at your profile begrudgingly think you can do it. Your innocence and lack of experience in this case might even work in your favor. If you get caught, you're not a hired operative. It's not an international incident. It works. And, mostly I guess, it's the only viable option with time running out and the need to do it now. There is no second choice. I need you to do it Justine. I'm asking and not even entertaining the idea you will say no."

None of what he says registers. I look at him in awe wondering how he knew all these years that I have always been playing a role to serve those around me. That's my takeaway and all that stands out.

CHAPTER THREE

Yes

I've been home for the last few hours. Pacing. Thinking. Swimming laps. I realize I'm not willing to walk blindly into a room full of people who, according to Robert, are not pleased with me as the operative. Is that what I'd be? Operative? Never a word I would have associated with my life.

I pick up the phone and call Robert. I tell him I'm coming back to speak with him *now*. I tell him I'm on my way and hang up the phone before he can say anything. I head out the door and try to put my thoughts and questions in order so I can decipher what's really going on.

He's in the library, dressed for dinner. I'm in sweatpants and my hair is still wet from the laps.

Figures.

"Robert, what's going on? What's this about? I can't walk into a room filled with ex-CIA and FBI without knowing more about what's going on and what you need from me. You have to tell me. Just you and me. I can't understand why you're involved in this."

He pauses. "You know who my daughter, Caroline, is right?"

Wow. Caroline. Of course. Everyone knows he had a daughter by his first wife who disappeared after she got off a plane in Europe while traveling with a girlfriend after high school graduation, never to be heard from again. But no one speaks of it.

Beth knew little about her or what Robert knew about what had happened. In all our years, I never heard him mention her. And Beth only spoke of it a few times. In all this time, come to think of it, I never heard anyone else mention her name.

"I know you have a daughter who disappeared," I reply. "Beth said Caroline went with her best friend to Europe and disappeared, like twenty-some years ago? She said you had done things, she didn't know for certain what, trying to find her. She thought it changed you, but she didn't know exactly how. She thinks it's what ended your first marriage. But I have no idea what happened more than that."

Robert stands up and walks slowly to a drawer in his desk, opens the drawer and pulls out a framed picture. He doesn't look at it. He walks over and hands it to me. He's in the picture, much younger and lighter maybe, not in stature but in the load he's carrying.

He is standing next to a willowy, smiling teenage girl. She's lovely. Comfortable with the camera taking her in, smiling, with her adoring father looking down at her. She looks, well, she looks smart, and she looks clear-headed and she looks confident. And she looks like she's fun to be around. She has that smile that says she has not a care in the world, but she is not oblivious to the world either.

I hand it back. He stands up, walks over and looks down at the picture as he places it back in the drawer. But he is gentle closing the drawer, which I realize says it all.

I wonder in that moment what he was like before this happened. It had never occurred to me that he might have had a larger capacity for empathy, or perhaps intimacy before he lost her. Immediately I realize what this whole thing is about and wonder that I hadn't already figured it out.

He walks back over and sits down next to me, but he doesn't look at me. He speaks to the space in front of him, and I have to lean forward to hear him.

"Caroline was picked up, probably right after leaving the airport in Rome, or that night at a party that somebody invited her and her friend, Sophie, to attend. They were both trafficked. To the Middle East. Saudi Arabia.

"The woman in federal custody may have information about who sold her to the Saudis. She may have been involved. I don't know if Caroline is alive or dead. I don't know. It took me decades to get this close to finding her.

"I have spent the last five years learning how it works and who does it. I have never stopped trying to find her. I am under no illusion that she is the person who I think of every day, but I want to find her, or at least what happened to her, no matter what I have to do.

"I was not well known back then. I didn't have the extreme wealth I have now. They wouldn't have picked her up if it was today. They target these girls. If she hadn't gone to Europe, they likely would have picked her up in the United States. It was not because she went to Italy that she was taken. It was because she was brilliant, beautiful and the kind of person that powerful men, psychopathic rich men, want to own.

"After these girls are taken, before they are sold to these monsters, they are groomed. The reprogramming can take anywhere from three months to a year. Depends on the girl and her strength of will. I'm thinking Caroline took a long, long time.

"I have spoken to some of the women we have rescued over the years, and the reason I keep pursuing this is because sometimes there is a piece of who they were, before the abduction, still inside. After years of therapy and sometimes medication, some of them come back. Not to who they were, but to something new. I believe in the possibility of a future for someone who has gone through this.

"The trafficker in custody, Ava Lloyd, was picked up by the FBI two days ago. My sources assure me that the men she deals with in the Middle East and in Russia don't know she was picked up yet. We have a once-in-a-lifetime opportunity to replace her with you. To have you go over there and uncover what I need to know, to shut down what we can and possibly find out what happened to Caroline. You will be Ava to them."

I don't say anything. For a long time. Finally, he looks at me.

"For the last year we have been looking for a way to pick Ava up and replace her. We needed to understand how it worked before we could do it. Then the FBI picked her up. We hadn't anticipated that. But we now believe that we have a full understanding of how it works.

"We thought we'd have more time to plan, to train you, or someone else. But we are out of time now. You can do this. You *will* do this, Justine. Not because of Caroline, but because someone has to, and I'm asking you to agree to have it be you. I will see you tomorrow morning at 6 a.m. in the guesthouse."

He stands up and walks out without waiting for my reply.

I sit for a minute, and then do the same.

Later, after I lay in bed too wound up to sleep, I think about Robert. How he is possibly more of an empathetic person than I thought. That he's observant. I think about what he said about me playing roles and wonder what he witnessed in me that saw that.

I wonder at the fact that he never moved on from the loss of Caroline, but he never spoke about it either, I assume to anyone. If he hadn't talked about her to Beth, I doubt he spoke about her to anyone.

I wonder at how he has taken these actions, all these years and has never given up. I always admired his business acumen, but I didn't know the depth of his humanity. I thought of him as mostly self-centered, but you can't be as observant about the motivation and makeup of others if you have no depth. I think maybe I like him more.

I finally roll over and sleep peacefully with the knowledge that this man is someone I want to work with. I want to make a difference, and possibly even save someone. The danger is no longer my primary concern.

CHAPTER FOUR

Nine Men and Me

As I drive over to the house the next morning, I listen to the radio, not thinking about anything. Then Tina Turner's *Simply the Best* comes on, and all of a sudden, I believe I can do this. I start to cry.

But then I start to sing at the top of my lungs. And I *know* I can do this.

By the time I walk into the room, though, all that bravado is gone. I feel sick. The sick to your stomach sensation you get when you think you're in big trouble but are compelled to face it head on.

Eight men, minus Robert, are seated around the dining room table. I immediately nickname them the disciples. I don't know any of them except for Chip, who runs security for the family. I meet his gaze and he smiles at me. All seem to be over the age of fifty, or maybe forty-five. Hard to tell. They are all white, have short hair, and scream government agency.

I wonder how long they've been on the payroll and what else, if anything, they do for Robert. I look each of them in the eye and shake their hands longer than they want, trying to let them know I'm paying attention. The trouble with this kind of bravado, though, is that you must back it up, and I have no way of knowing how to do that.

I feel totally out of place, and I immediately begin to question Robert's judgement in wanting me to be the one to go over and turn this nightmare upside down. One of these things is not like the others, and it's me.

I'm not Clarice Starling. I'm the ex-wife of an investment banker, a friend of the family. I'm a semi-retired B+ tennis player, and someone who people like to have at dinner parties.

I think about the fact that I'm none of the things needed for what I'm about to do; or at least my fantasy of what I'm about to do. I realize I have no idea about what it might entail, and like the self-help books have taught me, the best thing I can do for myself is not project but just be in the moment.

Silence the negative voice in my head that is in fear and flight mode.

It's one thing to be a chameleon at a dinner party, or political event. It's entirely another to wear the persona of someone you have no idea about how they think. *What* they think.

I know that every one of the men at the table thinks it's a catastrophic decision on Robert's part. I know this because they don't look at me. It's like when an accused man walks into the courtroom to hear the jury's verdict, and no one looks at him. It means he has been found guilty. I'm guilty as charged; not qualified for the task at hand. Sentenced to failure and possible damage to those they are trying to save.

There are two open chairs, one at the head of the table and one to the right. I take the one to the right. Everyone starts looking at the papers they have in front of them in three-ring binders or looking at their phones. There are two additional binders in the center of the table, one for Robert and one for me I assume, but no one hands me mine. No one looks at or speaks to me. I take out my phone and start scrolling through emails pretending to be engaged, putting on a show of calm.

Robert walks in and sits down at the head of the table. He doesn't say hello. As I suspected, his binder and mine are now handed to us. Okay, I get it gentlemen. Point taken.

"I assume you've all met Justine. Let's go around the table and introduce yourself and your role in the operation. John?"

Robert turns to his left and John says, "I introduced myself to Justine when she came in. Justine, I'm a specialist on the Middle East and Ben next to me is the same for Russia. We will prep you on what the political and cultural climate is in those arenas and how it could affect you."

"I'm Scott. I work with Chip, who I understand you know from his job around the family's security. We are in charge of your security and all your back-up technology and communication. We have time with you later today, and possibly on the plane on the way over if we need to."

Chip speaks next. "Justine and I have traveled together on family vacations and trips and have spoken often. I manage the technology and security group."

The next man, whose name I don't remember from the trip around the table when I arrived, doesn't say his name. He looks at Robert, not me, and says, "I'm ex-CIA and I'm running the operation strategy. You will be executing the plan my team puts together. My team will be working with you most of the afternoon and evening to prepare you for approaching the operation with what you need in order to execute what you're asked to do."

Time for me to step in. "I'm sorry. I don't remember your name." He looks away and says, "Jason."

I recognize that Jason is not on board with me as the Clarice of this operation. Hell, *I'm* not on board with me in this operation. I can't fault him. I think about how I should handle this and then bring myself back to the introductions. Pay attention to what's in front of you, Justine.

There is Jim, who is tasked with logistics. Sam, psychiatric consultant, who, based on how he introduced himself, isn't someone I would tell one thing about myself. And Harold, who is going to be my liaison for whatever I might need around anything that comes up.

Robert turns to me and says, "Justine, these men know you from the analysis put together by their teams on what we are going to do, what *you* are going to do. You will be infiltrating the tightly secured organization that was run by a woman named Ava Lloyd who was recently picked up by the FBI. She alone orchestrated the transactions but had people working with the women after they were picked up. Those people are also being held in custody.

"As far as we know, Ava's contacts never saw or spoke with her in person. It was all done through email, texts and phone calls.

"She sold girls, young women, to the buyers, wealthy and powerful men in the Middle East and Russia. We hope to replace her with you in a way we are still finalizing. We will then have you go to the Middle East to see if you can get some intel on what happened to Caroline. Where she might be, if she's still alive. The first time you go in will be to assess the situation and to establish yourself as trustworthy."

Robert takes a breath and looks at a paper he brought in. I don't think he needs what's on the paper. I think he's fighting his anxiety about speaking aloud the possibility that what happened to Caroline might be unveiled over the coming weeks.

He looks up and goes on, "Once we

understand how it works, we will decide what comes next.

"We know what we think the scenarios will be and have operational plans ready to finalize depending on which are in place, but I don't want to go into that now. You don't need more than the enormous amount of information you have coming your way this morning and over the next three days before you leave on Thursday. We decided last night that Thursday should give everyone enough time to get you ready and to put a plan in place.

"We pushed it back a few days. There is too much for you to do to get ready any earlier. You will be in touch with Ava's Saudi contact today through text messages, but you don't leave to see him until Thursday. You have a schedule that Harold will go over with you right after this meeting. There is a lot to do before you leave. Jason and his team will meet with you this afternoon and everyone else is on your schedule as well."

My mind wanders to the call with my friend, David, last night. He had gone over questions I should be asking, and I try to remember them now. He's an old friend I worked with and rented a house in the Hamptons with one summer before I married. He's a professor and teaches at George

Washington University about all things Middle East. Smart and alone in the world. He has a small posse of friends, and I count myself among them. I trust him. He has zero interest in gossip and will not pass on anything I discuss with him to anyone. I'm sure of it.

As expected, and maybe why I called him, he didn't tell me not to do it. He told me to not *react* to anything. He told me to marinate in what I think and pick my conversations and confrontations carefully. Truth is, so far anyway, I'm stuck on Jason. Already he seems to me to be the most important person in the room. And he still refuses to make eye contact.

They keep speaking and a few minutes pass. I have no idea what they just said. Focus, Justine. Take that scattered brain and keep it here. This time you can't hedge. You must know everything they are saying. I think of maybe asking them to repeat what they said, but I realize that would not bode well for what I think is still me making a good first impression. I lean forward and pay attention. Jason is in the middle of explaining some of the operational details.

"We have everything set up for you, Justine. You'll fly to Geneva where you'll open up an account with five million euros for expenses. You'll be able to wire transfer funds for any real estate purchases we need you to make. You will also have three credit cards and all your paperwork will be under your new name, Ava Marie Lloyd.

"Ava's history and backstory, including paperwork and anything that could be turned up about her will seamlessly trace back to her date of birth. Ava has no family or personal relationships that we have uncovered. She has never been seen by the people she does business with in Saudi Arabia and on the flight over you will listen to tapes we have of her doing business on the phone with them so you can hear how she presents herself. Your voice and hers are a fine match and no one should notice the difference when you arrive.

"We have listened to more than thirty hours of her on tape and there is nothing personal discussed on any call so we do not believe you will be called out to have information you won't have. No one does anything outside of the transactions to buy these girls and each transaction is set up the same exact way. She speaks to one person, Tariq, and we will go over what we know about him later. Jim will walk you through logistics now for the travel."

I stop them. "Wait. If she's been doing

business a certain way without meeting anyone, why am I changing that now? Why is Ava going on this trip?"

He stops and finally looks at me. I'm not sure it's respect, but maybe curiosity? "The Rainer administration could care less about this. They know about some of it, but not specifically about Ava and her operation. It's worse than a blind eye; someone high up is on the take. But the Justice Department had Ava in their sights during the prior administration and are completing this operation approved long before Rainer came into office. The Rainer people don't know that Ava's been picked up, and hopefully won't. And no one over there will share it with them either. It's been run by an isolated cell on a need-to-know basis for years.

"There's a Russian faction that also deals with this group, and it's thought that they're backed by the highest Kremlin officials, at least financially.

"So, you're going over under the guise of setting up new protocols under this new, 'more friendly' administration and to negotiate increased inventory and changes in deliveries.

"You're also trying to set up your programming center there, rather than in the U.S. where you would have to pay the Rainer people, or at least have them involved, which you are unwilling to do. You're going there to negotiate moving your business to Dubai, which will be better for them and you."

Alrighty then. Dubai. Tall buildings that Tom Cruise scales for fun is all that comes to mind.

Jim leans forward and we move on. "Justine, your jet will be at Palm Beach Airport at 5 p.m. Thursday. Rich and Henry will be the pilots, hopefully for all your flights over the next few weeks. They are retired from the airlines and will not be aware of the reason for your travel. They think you're a consultant working for high-net-worth individuals flying around looking for real estate, art and connections for business dealings.

"We have a full wardrobe packed for you that you can look through later. We can replace anything that doesn't fit if you need us to."

My head is reeling. How long has this plan been in the works? What questions should I be asking? I feel exposed, like someone's been watching me for a long time and I've been oblivious. I try to calm down.

Channel Clarice, Justine. She is the woman in your mirror. She's what you see looking out the window into that which you aspire to be. And I think about how pathetic it is that I'm channeling some film character to model my behavior. But it's not. I stop and remind myself that I'm doing the best I can, and I'll continue to do that. If Clarice Starling is the mentor in my head, that's just fine with me. No one needs to know.

The next hour is filled with information about what's going to happen and the coming day's itinerary, which if you ask me, should have taken several months or even years. I ask questions and take notes in my three-ring binder.

Robert turns to me. "You have the plan. Two things need to happen now. After Harold goes over the schedule, you need to work with Sam, and then lunch with me. And for the rest of the day, it's Jason's team to go over the operational plan and contingencies for possible scenarios already considered."

Sam had introduced himself as a black ops psychiatrist, whatever that is. He will educate and advise me on tactics for not being detected and how to assess the people I come into contact with.

Robert looks at me, and I find that I'm trying not to tear up. I know that if he is gentle in any way right now, I will be in a heap, so I look away and say nothing. I'm a crier and I realize that can't be a good thing in my new line of work.

I'm a photographer. I take pictures of people. Mostly their faces. Portraits. I look around the table and think about how in other circumstances, I would love to shoot this crowd. Interesting faces that the camera would capture with a unique perspective. Those are the fun faces.

Robert continues, "You will also be buying a safe house for us to use in Riyadh and possibly one in Dubai. We want them to see what you're doing, which we believe will give them some security that you're not running out. You will put them in Ava's name, and you will transfer the funds to pay in cash.

"We want you to find an apartment in a busy neighborhood and a building where people come and go a lot, so no one notices our people coming and going. Jim has some places already set aside for you to look at when you're there. Then if we need to increase our presence there, we can."

Chip looks at me across the table. Chip has kept us safe when we traveled together in the past and the kids like him, and so do I. He holds up his hand to stop the dialog, and I'm pretty sure he knows I'm struggling.

"Justine, I know you don't know anyone else

at the table. These are good guys and we all have your best interest as we go through this together. I'm going to go over the security parts for you now, okay?"

I nod, not looking at him.

I turn to Robert. "Please ask everyone to leave so you, Chip and I can speak privately."

Robert nods and everyone files out.

"Listen, Chip, you need to tell me if I could die over there or what the hell is my risk factor. We need to talk about me and my son, Michael, now."

Chip says, "If I'm worried about anything, and I can't say that I am, it's that you will be arrested and used as a political pawn with headlines around the world saying you were in there running a trafficking operation and the new administration uncovered it.

"They would love to make you a pawn and attack Robert's liberal politics. To be honest, that was one of the concerns from the group. Not that you *couldn't* do it, but if you are caught, all roads lead to Robert, which is worse for you. And for him.

"With the Rainer government wanting to side with anything from the Middle East arena, you will get no support from our government, and we will not be able to protect you. That's the real risk as I see it."

"What about Michael?" I ask. "Should I discuss this with him before I go? His mother is arrested in Saudi Arabia and he thinks she was there taking pictures for a client looking at real estate? Talk about thinking your whole life is a lie."

Robert grabs my arm. "No one can know what you are doing. No one. As we discussed earlier, say you are going to Saudi Arabia for a client. There won't be any issues."

No one can know. David knows. Well, you have your secrets Robert, and I can have mine. I have no doubt that David will never speak of this to anyone, but I need my own advisor and you have eight just in this room. David is my secret. I also want someone who is only on Team Justine to know the truth. Just in case. I will ask him to speak with Michael if anything happens and make sure he knows how this came to be.

I can't help but add, "With all due respect Robert, *we* aren't doing anything. *I'm* going on a plane with pilots who have no idea what's going on. By myself. I have no training and I'm not a brave person, or at least I haven't ever done anything brave. So, it's me who is going to do this.

"And I am going to do it. I decided that yesterday. I will do it, but I need to make arrangements around Michael, and I have things to do before I go. I have to update my will. I have things to take care of so my mind will be free to do what you want me to do. I think I should go home and do that and start on all this tomorrow."

Robert looks at me and picks up his cell. He dials and puts William, the lawyer who handled our family trusts and estates, on speaker. I stopped using him after the divorce.

"William, Justine Hollister is here with me. We need you to get her a new will and it has to be done in the next four hours. Get someone out here."

William says something I can't hear and Robert turns to me and says, "Does William have your will?"

"No, I don't use him anymore."

"William, I'm going to put her on the phone and she will tell you what she wants. It won't be complicated. It has to be done in a few hours."

He hands the phone to me. I look pointedly at him and go to the sliding glass doors, step out onto the patio, and sit down on a chair.

"Hey William."

"You okay, Justine? Are you sick?"

"No, Robert is just trying to help me out."

"You sure?" I know he doesn't believe me.

"I'm sure. Everything goes to Michael. He can be the executor of the will now. He's old enough. I should have changed that anyway, and my friend, Sharon Keavney, gets the locked trunk in my bedroom and she knows what to do with what's in there. My college roommate Lisa Kemper gets $25,000 a year for the rest of her life. Michael can give it to her; oversee it or whatever. That's it. I'll text you everyone's addresses."

My past will had no trusts but it had a lot of instructions around my belongings and little things that I realize now are a joke. I also realize I don't need to make a new will at all.

"Okay, Justine, I will have someone from the Palm Beach office come over there in a few hours to execute. It's 10:15 now. The updated documents will be there by two. Look, if you need to talk to someone, you know I'm here, right?"

"Of course. I'm good, William. Thanks. Bye."

I go back inside and everyone is there. They bring out the phone I will be using and I'm impressed. One stroke from me and it deletes everything. No one can get inside this little marvel and if they try, it deletes. I set the codes with nine digits and go through it all. I can send emails from it which will be encrypted, and anyone emailing, calling or texting me is deleted immediately afterward. There are other toys too, and I'm grateful that I'm a tech savvy girl, because my head is starting to spin.

We finish up. Everyone leaves and Harold stays and goes over my itinerary and some to-do's that are on me. It's complicated, but clear and well planned, even looking at it from my vantage point of not knowing how any of this works.

He's talking about how I drive to Palm Beach airport into a hangar (picture and diagram are in my notebook), but the way I get there is not a direct route from my house but goes by a back road route where they will make sure no one is following me with an overhead drone.

They'll enter the house a few hours after I've left, posing as a cleaning service and remove my computer, iPad, and any papers that shouldn't be seen by the world. I will leave them all on one table. They will return them when my wheels hit the ground upon my return. This will happen every time I go. I wonder how many times that will be.

"Harold, why are you doing that?"

He pauses, "I think you should ask Chip about that."

"I'm asking you. Let's save some time here because we are a little overscheduled."

He says, "I think it's in case you get picked up and the authorities come to the house. They want to limit exposure of you personally. Or that's what I think. Ask Chip, Justine, okay?"

He seems to want to say more but doesn't. We finish up and he heads out the door with a list of some things I've asked him to get for me to be able to do everything he wants.

Robert, Chip and I go to the main house to have lunch. There is a smattering of guests left over from the weekend looking at us and we sit at a table by ourselves. I think it makes us stand out, but when I point out that it might be better to sit inside, Robert answers, "I like sitting outside." It reminds me of someone once telling me that Robert's fatal flaw is that he tends to see things only from the perspective of how they affect him. At the time, I remarked that it seems to have served him well overall, but now I wonder.

Going over the plan with Jason is next on the agenda, after I examine the clothes they have for me. I can see this entire operation is a

well-oiled machine and I trust Robert to have
left nothing undone. That is why he is who
he is, and I'm grateful in this moment for his
brilliance and his strength and his thorough
approach to this operation.

Actually, I'm pretty sure for one brief second,
I'm grateful he wants me to do this. I'm almost
excited. The feeling is gone as fast as it appears, but
it does show up and I'm grateful. Then I remember
I'm the one cog in the wheel that has no experience
in this area and doubt sets in again.

CHAPTER FIVE

Get Some Sleep

After lunch, I walk into the cottage and Jason is at the table on his phone alone. I sit down across from him. He looks up briefly and then down continuing his texting and says, "We will be ready in a few minutes."

I sit and think about what I should do next. My instinct is to take out my phone, but I know that I need to fix this. I can't do this without him. If he isn't committed to the plan, then how can I be?

"Jason, can you please put your phone down for a minute, or ask your team to wait until you and I have some time together before they come in?"

He looks up and sets his phone on the table. His eyes stare at me just below my eye level. At least that's where I think he's looking. It's hard to tell. It's more than disconcerting. It's scary.

I continue, "I'm not sure if you don't like me after meeting me. Maybe you took an instant dislike to me. Or maybe you think lives will be lost because Robert has me doing this operation or whatever it's called. Maybe you are just someone who hates women doing things you think men should do? I have no idea, but I know you don't like me and don't want me to be here."

I pause to let that sink in. "I'm also sure that you are the link that will decide whether I get through this or not. If I can't work out some relationship with you that makes me feel like you'd like me to return at the end of this unplanned vacation, I won't feel safe. So, we need to talk this out or I'm going to tell Robert I'm out. I will not tell him why because I don't want to interfere with what you do for him, but I will walk away. It's up to you."

That was it. Not another word from me, I vow, until he speaks.

He looks down at his hands spread out on the table. I consider that perhaps he's trying to decide how much to tell me.

He looks up and starts to speak.

"I think Robert is making decisions based

on fear. I think he's worried that the window of opportunity is closing. I do not think it is, and I do not think you are the right person for this job. I never have, and we have been looking at the possibility of you doing this for months. I think you have a charmed life, have lived a charmed life, and you do not have the tools necessary to take risks that you will need to take to pull this off.

"The biggest danger for any agent is inertia. Being in danger and knowing it and then being unable to act. Sitting in what we call the X space, where the person who is onto you or attacking you has you covered, and you don't move. You sit there. It's a natural reaction that likely goes back to prehistoric times, but it doesn't work in undercover operations. It takes months of training to get your body to respond in the immediate moment in order to be safe. To plan your reaction when you walk into any room anywhere. To notice the small things." He pauses, "The small things, all the time. I doubt that you do that. Have ever needed to do that.

"You're the wrong person for this operation. I have a woman who was CIA undercover who can do it, but she's on assignment and won't be available for more than a month. Robert will not wait. I think he thinks the window will close in days. I think we could cover that and keep it open while we wait for her. I have no idea why he wants you over her. He has since the beginning.

"It's nothing personal, although I suspect you and I would never run in the same circles. So, you're right. I don't like this at all. I think the margin for failure goes up the minute you walk in the room. But make no mistake about who I am, Justine. If I'm here in this room, you will have the best plan and consideration I can provide. Trust that. And I will do everything I can to give you what you need to get it done."

I say nothing. And then three people walk in. He raises his eyebrows, signifying "your move." I stand up and walk over to the group and introduce myself.

We go all afternoon, and through dinner until midnight. I'm exhausted, exhilarated, confused, terrified. On the breaks I ask myself why Robert isn't going with Jason's first choice. I would. I ask myself why I'm not running? Jason tells me I'm a danger to the success of the operation, and I'm still here?

It's not just trying to figure out why Robert wants me that goes through my mind. It's not upset around what Jason has said and the danger it brings to the possible outcome. It's *why* I'm not afraid by what he said. It's *why* I'm more determined than ever to do it.

During one of the breaks, it hits me.

As everyone leaves the meeting and heads to their rooms to sleep before we go again tomorrow, I ask Jason to stay behind. We stand inside the door and he shuts it, I assume for security reasons.

We each take a seat and I look at him.

"I've been thinking all afternoon about your question around why Robert wants me for this operation. I have a theory and I want to share it with you, and only you.

"Every major thing Robert does, he's there and he's in charge. Buying stocks. Investing in deals. He's not a delegator. The things that matter to him have his total attention and are within his control as much as possible. Even where he takes the kids on vacation, he sets the destination, schedule, and every detail in between.

"Robert must believe Caroline is alive and we will end up attempting to rescue her. He wouldn't be doing this if he didn't. But when it comes time to go in and get her, he knows he won't be there. Can't be there. That is not the way he does things.

"Robert knows that most of the people

around him are there because of his money and power, or maybe even a love of risk and danger. Or maybe you're all motivated by good versus evil. I don't know. He doesn't trust many people in the best of circumstances, when there is no risk.

"I was around before he was the larger-than-life person he is now. After he and Beth got divorced, we remained close. My son, Michael and I traveled with him and his boys. He knows I'm committed to my son and to his sons. He trusts that. So, he wants the person in the room to be someone who won't leave without her; not hired guns who can justify whatever happens and not think twice about it.

"I think he has me going because, in his mind, I'm the next best thing to him. I want to say it again; he wants someone who won't leave without her. I think that's the reason. And I agree with you. It's probably a bad decision based on fear. And I agree with him. If she's there and we go in, I won't leave without her."

I pause and realize that saying it out loud is also admitting it to myself. I feel, well, I feel taller. I feel proud. Maybe I've found a piece of myself I never thought to examine or appreciate.

"One last thing. I don't know why but what

you said makes me want to do it more. Wants to show you who I am behind what you consider to be a pampered life. Maybe, just maybe, I haven't had the opportunity to be the kind of person you would prefer on this project. So, I'm going to do it. And I believe you'll do everything you can to help me succeed and I'm glad you're here. I thank you for this day and for your honesty earlier."

I sit there, and he thinks for a moment. He looks up and says, "Thank you for telling me. Get some sleep." He stands up and walks out of the room.

I take a breath, stand up, and follow him out. As I walk to my room, I have a calm clarity. I fall into bed and am asleep before I can reflect on any of it.

CHAPTER SIX

Peking Duck Tacos and Seaweed Salad

Four days later, I arrive at Palm Beach Airport an hour before we're due to take off. I know there are four disciples who are going to meet me to go over the plan one more time, with the changes that I know are being made right up until I leave the runway.

I'm not scared. I'm tired. I've lied to everyone I had to cancel plans with, and in the height of the season in Palm Beach, it was more than a few dinner parties.

The only person I confided in was David, who was more than supportive. He listened without comment and told me he thinks I can do it. I love him. He also will speak to Michael if anything happens, and that gives me a lot of comfort. I know I should tell them I told David, but I don't want him in jeopardy, and I trust him. That is enough.

Last night I went by myself early to Imoto at Buccan for dinner. Peking Duck Tacos, Lobster Potstickers, Seaweed Salad. Perfection. I asked to be seated in the corner in the back, rather than up front where I normally sit.

As I sat there and thought about the week, I realized the most challenging part of it all was lying to everyone. How it made me feel totally alone in a way I never do.

I'm a good liar. My parents were good liars. They never used the truth when a lie would put them on what they deemed "higher ground." Their higher ground was what they wanted to accomplish, rather than the truth, or what they actually thought. So, I know how to do it. I've spent a lifetime trying *not* to react with a lie, and for the most part, I've been successful.

Jason's team reinforced what I knew about lying. You have to keep as close to the truth as you can, and you have to remember every lie. So, what I told everyone was that the trip was for a client and I couldn't talk about it. All true. But when you think that those you care about might not ever know what happened to you, or that you could hurt them with a disappearing act that could never be explained, it weighs heavily.

Michael was the hardest.

"Wait, where are you going?" He had asked me more than a little confused.

I told him I had to go to the Middle East and maybe Europe for a client. I could be there a week, maybe longer. That the client is looking at property and wants me to take the pictures. Not sure why.

I had added in the Europe part because I wanted to have leeway should I need it. And, if it turns out I have to go back and forth more often, since there was discussion about moving some of the team including Robert to Europe to facilitate the operation.

"What client? What are you doing?"

"You don't know them," I had explained. "They do acquisitions and take in investors for each project. They need the imagery for the proposals. It's all on the Q.T. I have no idea how long it will take, or even the itinerary.

"I might miss your birthday. And I may be out of range in the Hinterlands. One of the properties is in some obscure Middle Eastern something or other, so I'll be out of pocket. I will text and email when there's a way, but don't worry. I'm sorry."

He will have to be on his own. It's safer that way.

I have an alias. Ava Marie Lloyd. Unlike many alias personas, Ava is a real person. They didn't show me a picture. They said I should picture myself as her mirror image and that showing her real picture would not help me. But they told me about her personality traits.

Such interesting adjectives they gave her. Dismissive. Confident. Passionless. Smart. Observant. Void of values. Soulless. They told me to take her traits and rename them for myself. I'm still working on it, but I like impatient better than dismissive, and I am that. Confident? I'm all in. Passionless I rename contained or guarded maybe.

Maybe I could like Ava in a weird way; not as a friend but more like if she and I were working together. I can see why it might be a fit. Except for "void of values." I'm not going to address that or be that. I may hide them, but I'm not giving them up.

I have a passport with her name and a picture of me. I know where I was born. I'm an only child. But I have no belief that I'm prepared for this the way a person should be prepared. I know they had to rush it because she had been picked up and they have no real window to have her disappear and reappear. They don't have the time to get me as up to speed as I should be.

But in the end, from what I gleaned yesterday, Ava never showed her personal self to these men in Saudi Arabia and Russia, and they never met her in person. So, I'm not as worried, even though I could see that the one time the team pushed me yesterday was in the section about becoming Ava.

I had thought it would be hard to become someone I've never met, but I listened to her diction and I think I get her. It's her voice that matters and according to the team, now that her contact will hear my voice in person, he'll be looking at me when I'm speaking and it's doubtful that he would pick up any difference.

I arrive at the airport and drive into the hangar as planned. I wonder if they are already in my house picking up my stuff. They will return the car to my driveway in the middle of the night tonight, just in case I don't return. The stuff from the house won't be brought back until my plane has landed when I return home. All the technology that tracks my car was removed during the week when I was with the team.

The removal of my things from the house is a thought that will fester. I have had a lot of those over the past few days. Thoughts that if I allow myself time in them, will put the fear of God in me in a way that could compromise all I have to do.

I walk to the Gulfstream. It's a plane set up for eighteen, but it's me, a party of one. My suitcases are there on the tarmac. I know what's inside. I board the plane with my soul and the clothes on my back. I realize this could be the moment when a panic attack sets in. The moment when I become Ava and leave Justine behind.

Robert took me aside last night to alert me to do whatever I think could make this a success, even if it's off script. "Justine, I want you to know that I will support whatever decisions you make. Do not be afraid to take risks if the rewards could lead to finding out about Caroline or meeting her. I will never criticize you for taking a risk. I will be disappointed if she slips through our fingers forever because you were not able to commit to a new option because you avoided the risk."

Late yesterday afternoon Jason drove me home before I went to dinner. I told him what Robert said. He didn't say anything, but I knew what he was thinking. He was thinking that maybe

I was right. That I would make a decision to save Caroline over anything, and a recruit from the CIA might not.

Jason and I have a new relationship. I can't say I've won him over, but the attitude is gone and I know I was right. He's the key to this whole thing. God, he's smart. Not funny at all; no personality. Who needs a personality when you think like he does? I'm grateful he's here, and I believe him when he speaks.

Just before we arrived at my house, he made a comment that will be with me in the coming days. "You have what you need to do this. I will be right behind you the whole way." I figure that's as good a pep talk as he's capable of, and I believe it's enough.

I'm ready and the plane takes off. I feel insignificant as the only passenger in what feels like a cavernous fuselage. And as we reach 35,000 feet, I know I'm alone.

CHAPTER SEVEN

Middle of the Night Dark

I wake up with a start. My watch says I've been asleep for four hours. It's dark, middle of the night dark.

This empty plane is hard to take. My thoughts drift to Payne Stewart, the golfer whose Learjet was climbing to the assigned altitude when it lost cabin pressure and all six on board were incapacitated and died due to a lack of oxygen. How our military flew alongside his plane looking for signs of life that were long gone by the time they realized the magnitude of what had happened.

So, it's dark, and I see Caroline's young innocent face from the photograph. My anxiety starts to soar. I'm breathing too fast and my heart is pounding. Fear starts to grow and I think I might never get home again.

My mind starts to spin through random thoughts that I haven't considered before now. I remember back to a time a month or so after I married H1. I woke in the middle of the night and ended up lying on the floor in the kitchen, twenty-nine years old, gasping for breath, sure I was dying of a heart attack.

But it wasn't a heart attack. It was my body telling me I'd made a terrible mistake and there were human lives involved that could get hurt, and I was desperate. I went into therapy and we divorced several years later. I tried after that to not wait until my body had to go into shock to recognize when I was on the wrong path.

But this is different. This is fear that I might die, or cause another's death; and that kind of anxiety is a protective mechanism when there is big risk involved. I start to breathe deeply to calm down.

Fuck the fear part of me. This is not an impulsive marriage decision. It's an opportunity for closure for many people, and possibly saving some women who are powerless over their own lives, their bodies.

This is a chance to do something with my life that matters. I remind myself that not everyone has the chance to do great things, and I'm lucky to be on this plane. Embrace the darkness, I tell myself.

I switch on the overhead lamp above my seat and start to make some notes, cryptically, but clearly laying out what I know and what I want and the steps in place to get there.

CHAPTER EIGHT

Justine, Clarice, C.J., Cristina

Geneva went well. I'm now on the plane with a million euros in a nylon suitcase. I've memorized all the people I will meet with and spend the hour before landing in Riyadh washing up and changing my clothes. I practice setting the burka perfectly around my face and like that it feels like a layer of cloth hiding a piece of the real me. Nice.

I take a break, grab a sandwich from the food laid out, and look out the window while I'm eating.

I think of my screen heroes. Of course, there's Clarice, who I never thought would have real parallels to my own life. But there's also C.J. Cregg from *The West Wing*, whose growth over the seven years in the series was something to behold, and to model. She was on the outside of the boys' network inside the White House and seven seasons later, she was leading them all. Sorkin writes his women as a bit clumsy, or inept when introducing them to us, and then they grow into the women they might have been all along. It's his only flaw in my studied opinion.

Lastly, there's *Grey's Anatomy*'s Cristina Yang, who strides to her own drummer, not society's model of how women should behave. I think she's head and shoulders above the other women on *Grey's*, especially when it comes to ethics, morals and courage. But the women of America embrace Meredith, silly self-centered Meredith, who is softer than Cristina, but nowhere near her in depth and character as far as I'm concerned.

I think about the qualities of all of them and how I want to take them with me on this journey. If I'm going to manifest success, I want to integrate the best of those characters into my persona. I know that I need to focus on being Ava with her horrifying list of traits; but to win I have to have some things about me that might not be obvious, but that will keep me safe, if that's an option.

To take what I watch over and over again and see if I can add it to my own DNA by sheer repetitive osmosis. It could happen. C.J.'s steady intelligence and ability to organize that which started out in chaos. And her muted humor. I love her humor. Cristina Yang's confident hand and commitment to excellence at all costs. And her extraordinary courage when she is in life-threatening danger. And, of course, the courage of my sister by another mother, Clarice, whose painful childhood set the stage for her drive to serve. It is she I relate to the most.

I think about how surprised I am at how brazen I was wearing Ava's armor at the bank in Geneva. How I looked everyone directly in the eyes and in a way that said, "Don't ask, and don't remember me." But it's not lost on me that Switzerland is a far cry from Saudi Arabia. But I decide that I should still celebrate the small victories and learn from what worked.

I spend the last half hour on the plane making up stories about Ava and her strength; and her fearless, though misguided, commitment to whatever she's doing. And I feel good. It's one of the tools that a member of Jason's team, a woman whose name escapes me at the moment, gave me. Practice scenarios in your persona. Watch yourself react in places you will find yourself. Build a history from which to continue to succeed.

I think about how they taught me to notice things. Notice people. Notice what is not "right" about them and remember it. I'm doing that, and I can see how interesting it is, and how it can get easier and easier, the more I do it.

One day last week after walking through the group at lunch at Robert's and heading into the cottage, Jason looked up and said, "Did you just come from the luncheon patio?"

"Yes, I did."

"What did you notice?"

"There was a man and I noticed he had a laptop in what looked like a dog carrying case and I wondered if there was a mesh place where a camera could be taking pictures.

"I noticed that no one looked at me with more than a passing glance, and Robert didn't look at me at all, but I know he saw me. I noticed that a thin woman had a hugely loaded plate and I wondered if she would eat it all and purge later."

He merely nodded. But for me it was a moment. I knew.

Rich walks back down the plane's aisle and interrupts my thoughts. "We are going to land in an hour Ms. Lloyd. There is a car waiting for you and the customs agent is coming on board to look at the paperwork. Is there anything else you'd like? I want to confirm that you have the right cell number for me so you can let me know when you would like to depart. We can be ready to go with a half hour's notice."

"Thanks, Rich. Please call me Ava."

Rich replies, "Thank you, ma'am."

I look at him for the first time. He's younger than me by maybe about five years. He's in incredible shape. He's handsome in an "I don't notice how cool I am" way. He's manly. I realize that I haven't known many manly men. I've known powerful men; powerful because of their stature in the finance arena, or because they're famous for something. Or rich. Like Arthur Ashe. Powerful. Sure-footed but not manly. Robert, oozing power and arrogance maybe, but not manly.

I like Rich. I like that he looks at me and doesn't mask that he's assessing me. It's not aggressive. It's natural. Friendly even. It invites me to look at him. And the way he moves on the plane? It's strong and sure and, well, it's safe. I like him. Or I have a feeling I would if I knew him.

"Call me Ava?" The anxiety around lying shows up again. I realize you have to think before every word, when every word you speak is a lie. I remember my father telling me when I was a small child that you have to be smart to be a good liar because the only thing that stays in your memory is the truth.

Funny, coming from someone whose truth was limited to whatever served him best, often having no resemblance to the truth at all. But I realize in that moment how right he was. Well, hell, I'm a smart girl. I will just have to slow everything down a bit.

We land and an hour later I arrive at the hotel. I'm staying at the Four Seasons Hotel Riyadh in the center of the city. It's a futuristic place, soulless if you ask me. It's amid acres and acres of New Age architecture, with a mall that is somewhere around 50,000 acres.

The hotel is right in the middle of it, and there's a soaring high "bridge" that people walk over through the entire area. I would never walk on that bridge. Afraid of heights. Snakes and heights. I take a moment to hope no one knows that about me. If you want me to talk, you could take me up on that bridge. I would never stay in this hotel on my own, but I can see it's smart. No one stands out here.

I'm in a one-bedroom suite and the first thing I

do after unpacking is sweep the room with a device that looks like a small flash drive. I've scanned the room for cameras, which I know I will do for the rest of my life, now that I know how often cameras are in hotel rooms.

It's early in the day and my meeting mid-afternoon with Tariq is in the hotel restaurant. I want to shower, maybe walk a bit and be calm when I go to meet him.

Tariq has been Ava's contact for years. He works for a powerful broker who is the mastermind of distribution for everyone making purchases in the Middle East. While it's not our understanding that Tariq is in touch with everyone purchasing these women, he certainly knows who they are. He is the one who delivers the women to the men who purchase them. He's the only one Ava sells through, or at least that we're aware of. Their correspondence is short and sometimes cryptic, but I understand it.

The thing I find most disturbing is the sexual preferences part. Based on the buyer's sexual preferences, the girls are taught what to do for optimum pleasure for their new masters. Masters? Owners? I hate both those words and wish there was a new word, one used for nothing other than this definition. Unique to the absolute horror and bile that overcome me when I think about it. My learning didn't include exactly what these preferences might include, but I can imagine. And I have.

Five hours later I walk into the restaurant where he is already seated, and I choose the seat across from him. Everything that I like about Rich is not part of Tariq. He is short and has a belly that sticks out more because he slumps. He looks at me and quickly away and his hands are fidgeting in a way that says he knows he is minutes away from having to do something unpleasant.

The photographer in me sees that if I shot him, I'd have to do it from an angle. Never straight on, dead center with him looking into the camera lens. I like shooting people that way, but he would never be honest enough to be seen from that vantage point. I would shoot him from the side without any engagement with the camera at all.

I don't shake his hand but I wait until he looks up and say, "All these years. Here we are." I do not say it's nice to meet you.

He launches right in. It's not that he's in a hurry. It's that he has been bottled up with it for the last few days since I said I was coming.

"Why are you here? I'm not sure this is a

good idea." His accent is noticeable but he seems comfortable conversing in English.

I wish I had the seat looking into the room instead of the wall behind him. It makes me nervous. I lean across the table, look at him and say, "America is changing. The presidential family's relationship with Saudi Arabia's ruling family is taking a new turn. One that will be better for you here for certain. The president's son-in-law is closely connected to the Crown Prince. In fact, President Rainer's first overseas trip was here to this city. It's unprecedented. And, while he was here, the son-in-law was told about the work you and I do which not only surprises me, it also angers me.

"Wealthy American men do not buy women this way and they do not want to know about who does. Especially American women. Was my information given to him? I thought there was distance between me and those who purchase what I sell. But it can't be changed. I do not believe I can email comfortably anymore. I'm not confident I can operate without scrutiny anymore. So, I'm moving my operation here and to Dubai."

I stop speaking. He says nothing for quite a long time. I let the silence hang there. For as long as he needs.

It's not that long.

"What about the two women you are delivering soon?" he asks. "We waited seven months for you to finish their training. They are already sold and the buyer is most anxious to receive. Where are they?"

I reply, "I will deliver them as promised. But this new development has set me back. I had to move them and will have to spend substantially more resources to get them out of the country safely. You have not answered me. Did you know the prince was telling anyone about our partnership? Who else knows? Why do they know?"

He answers, "I did not know. I don't know the answers to your questions. I will find out and will meet you again. What do you want to do now?"

I reply, "First of all, you will have to pay me more for what you have ordered. I have to pay out money that was never planned. Twenty million euros more to move the operation, in addition to the four million for the two girls. I'm moving my headquarters and training program to Dubai."

I give him the cell number they gave me. "You can text me at this number. I will stay in Riyadh until I hear back from you."

As he leaves, I wish I could check out the

room, seeing everyone without looking at them the way Sam taught me. I wait fifteen minutes; it feels like an hour. I eat part of the salad they had set on the table right after I sat down and head out the door. I don't look back or around. I can do this. I can do this.

I decide to walk outside for a few blocks, get some air. It's crowded and ugly. People are all well dressed, hurrying on their way without a thought of me walking along. Normally I would have looked in windows, checked out the local flavor, but Ava would never do that and I realize I know that intuitively. I only walk five blocks and then walk back. There is nothing I want to explore here.

I arrive back at the hotel, access the computer in the lobby and do my trick to log in as someone no one can track. I send a coded message that I have made contact and shut it down.

I wonder where the pilots are staying. Should I have asked? I text Rich and ask him where he's staying, and he says somewhere near the airport without giving me the name. Strange.

I go to my room, turn on CNN and wait.

Two hours later I get a text from Tariq.

Added euros ok. No answer for other questions. Tell me next steps.

I text back that I will be in touch and text
Rich to get the plane ready to go to Dubai.

CHAPTER NINE

Apartment on the Top Floor

I buy an apartment in Dubai in three hours. It's on a busy street, the top floor, a terrace with panoramic views in all directions. It's the first one I see. I don't bother visiting the others. I wire the broker five million euros to be transferred the next day. Everything that is in the apartment stays. It's three bedrooms and 2,800 square feet, and I'm good with it.

No one will notice strangers coming and going. It's an international crowd of owners and I'm confident many of them, like me, will be in and out. It feels as if not many live here full time and I doubt it's filled with families.

The best part is that it's located on the top

floor. I can get on the elevator, wait for everyone to choose their floor, and then select a floor higher than everyone else's but not the top floor. That button I will push after everyone leaves the elevator.

I'm supposed to contact our team in Dubai but I don't want to. I don't have anything to plan with them yet, so why expose myself to anyone until I have something to say? No, I'm not going to set that up. I pause after deciding to skip connecting and realize it's my first deviation from the plan. I wait a few minutes before sending a text to Harold telling him to let the team know I will not be meeting with them.

Immediate response. *Why?*

I don't answer him. I don't know why. Did I think once I was in the field, I'd call the shots without accountability?

Should he have asked? I start to doubt myself.

I send a text to Tariq.

Will be back in Riyadh tomorrow morning. Meet me same place at 11.

I let Rich know we will have wheels up early tomorrow morning to head back to Saudi Arabia. I let the Mothership know as well.

I walk around the hotel neighborhood and think about how cold extreme Middle Eastern wealth is. How the architecture doesn't make sense, it just looks expensive and big. Slick. Shiny. So many windows. It has no soul. No foundation. I eat in the hotel restaurant and ask for a corner table with a view of the room. It's quiet and I'm calm and comfortable. I head back to my room to sleep.

CHAPTER TEN

Doorway In

I sleep well. I wake up and take a moment
lying there to go over the last few days. It's only
been a week since Robert asked me over the
backgammon table to do this. It feels like a year. I
feel more alone than I ever have, but I think about
the fact that I don't feel lonely. I feel on edge, but
not in an uncomfortable way. It's almost like a
wakefulness that I've never had before. Is that even
a word? Wakefulness.

On the plane back to Riyadh, I think about
the best way to get the information needed to
infiltrate and destroy the network that services these
men's power-based sexuality. It repels me.

Something tells me to keep vigilant and open

to anything, and to expand on what I learn. I know that the meeting with Tariq is mine to control and I think it might provide the opportunity to emerge better connected. I'm not wrong.

Sitting at the restaurant later, I confirm with him that I'm moving my portion of the organization to Dubai. He seems hesitant and I decide to ask him why.

"You seem to have something on your mind? What is it?"

"I sent you a message two weeks ago. Why didn't you answer?"

"I don't know. What message?"

"Message that was sent to the other email address. I didn't hear back. I thought that is why you came here."

"I did not get it. Actually, I'm not sure it even came through. We have put new software in and changed some things because of the new interest from the government in what I'm doing. It might have been deleted. I can check to make sure it won't happen again. We will set up a new email address. Don't email to that address again. What did it say?"

He looks at me and I think he is deciding whether or not to answer me truthfully. A red flag was turned on by the fact that I didn't see his email.

An email address our team doesn't know about? I know instinctively not to ask more about it.

"Problems with some of the girls," he continues. "We think they are sad. We don't know what to do. One of the older ones is talking to them. We want you to meet her to decide what to do."

"What do you mean 'sad'? And which woman?" Of course they are "sad." They are in the depths of hell and falling apart, you ridiculous excuse for a human being.

"They stop talking to the other women and masters," he says. "Some are not doing good. We leave them alone. But it's not good. You must fix it. One is becoming a problem."

He hesitates and I can see he's trying to decide whether to answer my other question. Patience. I sit there looking at him trying not to appear too interested, but still letting him know I want to know which woman is trying to help.

"She is a woman brought in many years ago. She is now a wife of the sheik. He trusts her. She knows some of the women."

"What are you talking about? She became a wife? How did that happen?"

"She is the only one," he replies. "I don't

know more. Her husband is a friend of the sheik who owns the woman who is a problem. She went to see her."

This was it. Just what I'd hoped to find. The doorway in.

"We have worked for years on the perfect programming to keep them on track," I say. "I want to meet with this woman and try to figure out what's going on. Maybe we need to take a closer look at this and touch base routinely after placement in order to quell this issue in the future for the others. I wish you had told me sooner. How long has this been going on?"

He looks at me and I know right away what happened to the woman. And I don't believe for a second there's only one. One is expendable. They must be concerned that this could become a real issue.

I continue, "I will have to give this more thought. How about I come in and assess what is needed and afterwards propose a plan to fix this. The first step would be for me to meet with the woman who has spoken to her. Can you arrange that?"

He thinks for a minute and I add, "You know, you should tell the men that you thought of it, and I said I could do the initial plan. Don't ask them for any money. I have an investment in each of these girls, and I'm disturbed by what you are saying. This is not good for any of us. I could be back here in a few days and begin. Let me know."

But I know instinctively they will jump on this.

I end the lunch, text Rich to have the plane ready in two hours, text the team that I am heading back and rush to my room to pack.

CHAPTER ELEVEN

Masterstroke of Subterfuge

I stand in front of the mirror at home in my bathroom and try to remember what day it is. How do I look after my first trip over?

It's not lost on me that perhaps more important than how I *look* is how I *feel*. I feel solid, but without a full plan; a plan that has to be flexible.

I've often asked myself if I'm like the *Titanic*, unable to change course in a timeframe that works, or like a jet ski, with the versatility to address in the moment whatever has come up.

My vote is the jet ski, idling in the middle of the ocean. Ready.

I haven't yet gone over with anyone what

happened with Tariq and the idea I pitched to him. No one knows about it, and I have a feeling that it isn't going to go over well with the disciples, especially Jason.

But I also think Robert will jump on it. It puts me inside, and I think he knows that without anyone inside, he has few, if any, options.

I'm nervous. Like I want to spend money that was targeted for groceries on a movie and popcorn and that I will be in trouble.

"Stop." I say to my inner voice. "I'm not a powerless girl facing a six-foot-three father with no agency. Stop."

I decide I'll go over it with Robert in person before we meet with the group. I think I'm right, and I'm ready to defend it. But it's new ground for me, and I'm anxious to get it over with. The last thing Robert said to me before I started out was, "Go with your gut, even if it's outside the plan."

I'm tired. Almost thirty hours in the air and multiple time zones in three days. And I'm pretty sure I have to go right back in. I'm heading over to Robert's to start the conversation around next steps. I text that I need to meet with him alone before the team gets together and finish getting ready.

I become more and more stressed as I drive over. I stop and clear my thoughts. I *am* a risk taker. I assume they assessed that part of me when they signed off on me. I have generally acted without pause, even with large decisions, and just as with all strengths and weaknesses, there are times it works for me and times it doesn't.

I get five minutes with Robert before we go in and he takes the news of my initiative and says nothing.

We walk into the meeting room and all are assembled around the table. Everyone is there. Robert presents what happened. They all start talking around me. No one is asking what I think. Some think my idea about getting on the inside of their operation is risky but possibly game changing. Others think it's too risky and possibly destructive to the overall mission.

I also sense that some of them are just furious that I think I have the power to make a decision this critical. The fact that I presented it to Tariq without consulting them is beyond my scope of authority. Jason says it first.

"Justine you could have told Tariq you would get back to him with a plan. That would have given us room for options. We are locked in now without the ability to change direction." He doesn't seem angry, but I'm sure he knows how to not seem anything.

I pause before answering. "Jason, Tariq was not happy that I hadn't seen his email to another address that apparently you all don't even know exists. He was distrusting of me. I had to make sure he believes I'm in charge. I wanted him to think about the option I was presenting, not that I didn't have access to a secret email address that is supposed to be in place."

There is a quiet moment and Robert ends it.

"I told her to do it."

Huh?

"I told her if she was given an opportunity or could create an opportunity to see any of the women, she should take it. We're going to proceed with her plan and Justine and I are going to the house for another meeting. Figure out next steps and we will meet again after lunch. She goes back in as soon as she hears back from Tariq. They will jump on this."

We start walking to the house and I ask him why he said that?

"You did what you did. Now we need to make it work. It's a waste of time to debate it, and time is my enemy right now. I actually like it and think it could work."

Then it hits me. If I'm on the inside, and if Caroline was in their network, maybe he thinks I will find out what happened to her. My mind starts wandering. I cannot raise suspicions by asking Tariq about anyone. I have to have no specific interest in any of the girls. My thoughts are interrupted by his next comment.

"You know you look like shit."

I ignore him.

"Who are we meeting with?"

"Thomas Coleman."

I say nothing. I remember meeting Colonel Thomas Coleman at a lunch a year earlier just before the election that put the joke of a president in office. Coleman was advising Robert about what might happen with our foreign policy after the election. I was at the compound for the weekend and happened to join the two of them for dinner.

"Why are we meeting with Coleman?" I ask.

"Because he is a brilliant strategist and I think we need him."

A few minutes later, Coleman walks into the room, and it strikes me that he has a soft way about him that I suspect is the perfect ruse. I hadn't liked him when I met him those years ago, and I'm sure I'm not going to like him in this.

I remember him as standing tall and that he seemed to love the weight of the many shiny objects he wore on his imposing chest when he was active. I think he liked the power they provided. I think he's a man who feeds his testosterone rather than channeling it.

We sit at the dining room table while all the guests are eating outside and I think it's much better than having them watch us. I realize no one knows Coleman is here, and I think that, in itself, is a masterstroke of subterfuge.

For years I've spent days at this house in the winter. I can't help but wonder at what else has been going on here while I was eating Ring Dings and talking to CEOs and college presidents.

Coleman likes what I'm suggesting. He thinks I can keep their interest alive and that it's a fast track to the inside track. He thinks it's the perfect hide-in-plain-sight scenario and I'm over the moon with the reinforcement of his approval.

Wait. Am I giving him creds without evaluating myself what I think of him? My exuberance at his approval is more about my ego and less about his thoughts. Truth is, he isn't saying anything that's all that insightful. While that in itself is not a problem, it also shouldn't make me euphoric or feel as if I've been validated.

We finish lunch and Robert and I play a few games of backgammon, which is just what I need.

CHAPTER TWELVE

Mistaken for a Barbie Doll

The disciples reconvene later in the afternoon with the addition of Coleman. He sits next to Robert in what has been my seat and I take a seat further down the table. I don't like it.

Robert speaks first. "Thomas, Justine, and I have met and we are all in agreement that she goes back as soon as she has their go-ahead. I want to reconvene tomorrow morning with a strategy from the team on what her plan might look like. Leave nothing unexamined."

He continues, but I sit there trying to figure out why I'm uncomfortable. I wait for an opening.

"Robert. I want some things added to the list. I want this group expanded to include women who've worked with survivors of trafficking. I need information I think only they can provide. How the victims are targeted, how they are groomed.

"What did Ava's people do to prepare these women? What should I expect when I meet them? If I'm given access to the women, I need to know what to expect and how to best serve them without adding to their trauma.

"I want to be there when they present. I don't want everyone here telling me their interpretation of what they were told. I want to hear from them directly. And, I think we should add at least two retired agents to this group who are women.

"With respect, I'm uncomfortable with the points of view that I hear coming from this group. I'm not hearing any empathy or what I consider to be true understanding of what these women are going through. I think it's a deficit, especially if I'm going to meet with one or more of them. I can't go back in until I understand exactly what happens to them from the time they are abducted until the time they are delivered. One of the women on the team should be someone who has been through it."

First there is silence, and as I look around the table, I also sense anger. This only strengthens my resolve. "I'm sure you will all agree that it was an oversight. That if this was an operation about breaking the POW camps in Afghanistan, you would never consider putting a plan together without first-hand experienced input." I look at Coleman. He meets my gaze and I don't see anger there at all. I see admiration.

I press on. "John you are a specialist in the Middle East. Ben, Russia. But no one on this team has any experience whatsoever in trafficking. I think it could help. It certainly couldn't hurt but if there was a reason this was overlooked, I'd love to hear it. If I might meet some of these women, I need to understand how they think."

John speaks. "Yes, I'm a specialist in the Middle East, and no I've never been trafficked, but I have spent countless hours over the last year as we were working on this, getting briefed on how it works and I can speak to it without adding another person to the room. It would change the working dynamic we have created and add a risk factor of yet another person knowing what we are doing. This is a mistake, and I resent your lack of respect for how I approach my work here and what I have brought to the table. I spent time with you prepping you on the Middle East, and I think it gave you everything you need to know."

Robert looks at me and I can tell he's not sure.

I look back at John and continue. "Really? If that were true, John, part of that time would have been spent on women in the Middle East and their role and their sexual place with the wealthy of Saudi Arabia. And unless I was in the ladies' room when you were presenting it, you never touched on anything about women there. And I'm not the wiser for it."

I turn to Robert. "Could I have a word with you and Thomas?"

Robert motions to the door for the others to leave, but before they do, Jason raises his hand and everyone becomes quiet.

"Justine is right. We will get a few people with experience right away."

I shoot him a glance, not a smile, because I know without reference that he wouldn't like that. Be silent Justine. Let him take it from here.

Everyone leaves the room. It's just Coleman, Robert and me.

Coleman pours me a glass of water, gets up and puts it in front of me. He sits down next to me and turns to Robert.

"She is right. And this same issue has been part of our failure in the military. We can have these women here by tomorrow morning and we will need one day to get it ready. But I have an additional idea. I think we bring in Ava as well and give her the opportunity to work with Justine. I can make this happen, with the same team that put together our inside team in the CIA that got us here."

"Wait," I say incredulously. "This was all done by you? You got the internal team together for the last year to give Robert access to all this information?"

Robert answers. "The last five years."

"Would they let Ava come here?"

"No," Coleman replies. "But I can get you in to spend time with her. I can fly down to D.C. with you and you can meet with her. I can't go in because everyone will wonder why I'm there. You can be doing a psychological analysis."

Robert shakes his head yes. "Do it. And, put the women Justine wants on this team. Justine and I are going to leave the room while you make this work with everyone else. It will go better if Justine isn't in the room."

He turns to me. "You shouldn't have done that with everyone in the room. You could have said it to us at lunch and let us put it in place.

They don't like that it came from you, and it has upset the balance in the team. Next time, run it by me first."

I'm not going to argue, but I recognize that the scene from *The Silence of the Lambs* when Jack Crawford removes Clarice from the room filled with police to quell the male bruised egos is being replayed right here, right now. But I won the war, I don't need to keep fighting the battle.

Robert and I leave and he walks me to my car. "Never put me in a position like that again. Never." He's not mad. He's just clear. I am good with that and I realize I don't need to give any ultimatums ever again. I have the strength to fight any battle one-on-one, and if I lose, I walk away head held high. This is new to me and I don't quite know how to manage it. But I need him to understand something, too.

"Robert, if these men think I'm the Barbie doll equivalent of a robot put in the field to execute their plan without any control, I will not be able to do what you want. They don't have to like me, but each of them, if they are as smart as you think they are, know that I'm right.

"This is the start to a road where they actually ask for my input, or at least treat it with respect.

And my input, if I'm the only one in the field, should be worth having. Right?"

He says nothing, but just as we get to my car he says, "No one would mistake you for a Barbie doll."

I'll take that as a yes.

CHAPTER THIRTEEN

Crying When You Swim

I wake up the next morning and decide to call Dr. Ryan. Although we have never met in person, she was introduced to me in the meetings before I went overseas as a therapist who works with CIA operatives on issues that arise from the work they do. The isolation, the fear, the terror after the fear is over, whatever psychological challenges operatives have that they can't discuss with friends and family, who often have no idea what they do. She is available to speak with me if I need her.

It seemed so alien at the time but not anymore. I'd called Michael last night and said I was back for a few days and we talked about what was going on with him but when he asked about my trip and what the hell I was doing, I was vague and boring.

It created a distance between us because I was still in it, every fiber of me, and he was like that voice you hear in the distance. I wasn't present. And I always strive to be present when I'm with him. I've often thought how lucky I was that there were no cell phones when he was younger because I'm quite certain I would have been that mother glued to her phone at the playground.

I dial the number and Dry (my nickname for Dr. Ryan already) immediately picks up. "Good morning, Justine. How are you doing?"

That was quick. "Good I guess. Who the hell knows, but I'm not calling about me. I'm calling about a few questions I have."

She is silent. I wait a few seconds and then continue.

"I've stepped into this male-dominated group and requested that they better prep me on the women who are trafficked and what it's all about for them. They are gathering the information now. I don't know how much you know about what I'm doing."

"I'm familiar with the overall work you're doing, but not the specifics. But you do not have to filter what you say. I think they explained that to you."

"Yes, well, I thought you might have insight into how traffickers take a young woman from a rich entitled background and turn her into a sex slave. Is sex slave even the term? Do you know how you program someone to make a life change like that and behave the way you want them to?"

"I'm sure you've heard of Stockholm Syndrome where hostages develop a psychological bond with their captors," she says. "You can start with that, but I think there's more involved here. The women you are dealing with are not chained to a bed in a dark room for years. They live in the lap of luxury, although sequestered, and it's more complicated than that.

"I can tell you that some have had the chance to walk away after years of being, let's use the term 'forced concubines' instead of 'sex slaves,' although both terms are applicable. Yet they've chosen to stay. The Stockholm proponents would say it wasn't a choice, that by then they were so conditioned to their life that they no longer had the ability to make an independent decision. I don't know. I haven't worked with any of these women, but that's the best insight I can offer."

"Thanks."

"How are you doing with all this? How is your confidence level?"

"You know it's funny you would ask that question. I think dealing with the group of men on Robert's team is harder than I realized it would be. But if what I hope happens next, happens, then I will be much more vulnerable, and I guess I'm not all that confident about that." After I say it, I surprise myself. It's true but hasn't been a coherent thought until I voice it to her.

"Justine, this will change you. The parts of you that need to do this, some of them anyway, have never been tapped before. It can be liberating, and it can be confusing, even frightening. The key is to think them through when you're having them and not react to them immediately, but don't ignore them.

"Viktor Frankl had a great thought about that. He said, 'Between stimulus and response there is space. In that space is our power to choose our response. In our response lies our growth and our freedom.' What I personally find most perplexing about it is figuring out when to respond, and when to let it go."

"Thanks, I will think about that." We both laugh at the idea that she is giving me a stimulus with her quote and I'm going to take some space to respond.

Then I add, "I'm changing. I've always cared more about what people thought than what I think. I'm a chameleon, trained by a father who wanted me to please, and I'm leaving that behind. I know, on some level, that here I have to do and say what I think, that it is key to keeping me safe. I don't have the luxury, maybe, I'm not sure of the word here, of relying on my ability to charm. The disease to please is of little benefit to me now."

She takes a moment. "There is a middle ground. Choosing when to use it rather than relying on it as your go-to will serve you best. It *is* a tool in your toolbox, and you are smart to determine when it will work for or against you. But it's only one tool. Not always your go-to tool. And, by the way, I hope you will take it home with you when you finish this because no one is ever served well by ignoring their true reactions."

We hang up. I get up and head to my pool to swim laps. I like swimming laps. As the years have progressed and I've gained weight and lost agility, swimming is a luxurious exercise that I love. I remember back when my father was training me to be a swimmer in our pool. He had me up every morning doing laps. A hundred of them. And he timed them and sometimes I would cry in the water because I knew no one would know how hard it was and how much I didn't want to be doing it. I also knew I could cry in the water because no one other than me would know I was crying. I highly recommend doing your crying when swimming.

At my first swim meet, I was swimming the backstroke. There were a few hundred people there. It was a qualifying heat and my coach said to just beat the others and not go all out. I started swimming and thought I was well ahead of everyone else and then I heard my father yelling to swim faster. Above the din of all those people, I heard him. I panicked.

I stopped swimming and stood up in the pool to look around while everyone swam by me because I thought I'd made a mistake. I was in the third grade. We never discussed it on the way home, and I never raced again.

But now swimming and gliding through the water under my own propulsion is a joyful experience. Truth be told, there are times you must listen to your own voice, not all the voices around you yelling at you to do it their way. I had no agency when I was in the third grade to hear my own voice. I can listen to me now.

I hear the ping of a text coming in. It's from Harold who says Coleman will meet me tomorrow morning at 8 a.m. at the airport to go to D.C.

I'm going to meet Ava.

CHAPTER FOURTEEN

I Don't Like the Earrings

I walk on the plane, stop to say hello to Rich and Henry and head back to find Thomas already buckled up and ready to go. I'm big on punctuality and Michael complains that I bred him to be a half hour early; and now he is constantly waiting for everyone else. I always told him it was better than having others wait for him. A few minutes to sit and think is a gift to yourself. I wonder how early Coleman arrived and if it's one of his power plays.

"Hello, Thomas. Thanks for setting this up."

He's all business. "No need to thank me. I think it's a good idea. Ava is being taken from her current location to a hospital for psychological evaluation. She was moved there last night. That's where you'll conduct the interview. You were brought in from no-one-knows-where because you're a specialist. You are Dr. Rachel Woods. And there's a profile online that says you are a doctor dealing in psychological evaluations of psychopaths."

He reaches under his seat and pulls out a backpack. "Here are a wig, brown contacts, some makeup and clothes for your disguise. I know you have been trained in recognition avoidance, but I will remind you to meet a gaze, but only briefly, and always keep your gaze lowered to avoid full camera recognition. I will not be with you. I'm going to wait on the plane until you get back, but I want to go over the strategy on our way."

"Okay."

"Your objective is to see if she is willing to provide information about how these women are conditioned. What traits do they look for when they're selecting their targets? What hasn't worked? What has?" He drones on.

The space between stimulus and response is my power. It was my idea to get information on the women and how it all works, and it was his idea to have Ava brought in, which I think was brilliant. But I realize he has no idea what information might be of interest to me. What do I want and need her to share?

I know what I want to know. I want to know her. I want to read her. See who she is and get some inkling of the why. I want to see if we can connect.

I also want to have her tell me how to read the people I will be trying to manipulate when I get there, not just the women, but also Tariq. How does she view him? Weaknesses?

So having no agenda and being able to adjust what I want and my expectations when I'm with her is how I want to approach it. No need to sell him on it. He won't be there.

He's finishing up, and I thank him and say I want to think it all through.

"Thomas, how do you get someone to talk to you in these situations? Why would she speak with me? I can't go in and just bombard her with questions."

"She will think by the time you come in that you have the power to help her situation, or not. That should make her want to be cooperative and answer your questions. You will only have two hours max. That isn't a lot of time, but this plan allows you to come back for additional time with her if we need it in the future."

He opens the front pocket of the backpack and pulls out a watch. "Put this on. When you walk in, look at your watch as if you're checking the time. When you put your hand down, click this button on the side and it will jumble any listening device in the room. There shouldn't be one, but I want to be sure."

"Does it tape our conversation as well?" I'm not sure I want it to.

"No, it doesn't."

Why don't I believe him?

I take the backpack and walk to the back of the plane and change my clothes, putting on what was sent right down to the earrings. I change my mind and decide to leave the earrings on the plane. Maybe there's a microphone in them.

I come back and sit down. It takes him five seconds before he says, "Justine, you forgot to put the earrings on. Go back and put them on."

I reply, "I don't like them. I don't want to wear them."

He says, "If you wear them people will look at them and not at your face. There is a reason for everything we give you."

I put them on, lean back and close my eyes. I think about who Ava is and why she is who she is. What brought her here? I have no idea, but I do think that she is one smart lady to have done what she's done. And I do not underestimate that it takes more intelligence to be dishonest, and even evil, than honest and good.

She is going to assess me, and she is going to respond in the way that best serves her and what I can do for her, not to be confused with the way that best serves me. I decide that I will leave the opening to her and see what I think.

CHAPTER FIFTEEN

Why are you here, Doctor *Woods?*

She walks into the room without looking around and sits down. She takes a moment, then raises her eyes to look directly at me. I think I catch her noticing the wig, but I'm not sure. She doesn't say anything. Neither do I.

I use the silence to study her. Taller than me maybe? Brown hair. Not noticeably attractive and hard to see what her look would have been because she's in a shapeless jumpsuit and slippers, and her hair is cut short. I wonder if they did it, or if she did.

I break the silence first. "Hello. I'm Dr. Rachel Woods, and I believe they told you I'll be evaluating you."

"Fine. Evaluate me." She meets my gaze and her eyes say it all.

"Okay, let's put the evaluation aside for a moment," I begin. "As a psychiatrist, I'm much more interested in the trafficked girls than I am in you. Although how you got here is immensely interesting to me. But maybe we can start with the girls."

She says nothing.

"On the way here, I thought about the young women who are taken and placed in this network and I couldn't help but wonder why a woman would do that to other women." No reaction.

"I also wondered what you look for. What qualities you care about in the girls you abduct."

She waits for a moment and then answers.

"I did it for the money. And, how we chose them? We knew beforehand what was wanted, the look, the disposition. The rest was random. You, for example, would never have interested us." She looks down at her hands and then back up at me.

I'm not sure why she added that. It's disconcerting, but I decide to let it go. It's so not about me.

"If I were you, Ava, I wouldn't tell me anything truthful. So, my job is to determine what your motivation is for whatever you're telling me, and then I can evaluate why you're saying what you're saying."

She looks at me with more interest. "I'm wondering why you told me that."

I think that's the truth. "I'm not sure why I told you that. But I don't think I'm giving anything away."

"I know I will never see the light of day as a free person again," she says. "What happens here today doesn't do anything for me."

"Well, you're right and you're wrong. I don't think you will ever leave the prison system. But what I think, and recommend, just might determine how comfortable you are as an incarcerated person. Not to be confused with the kinds of restraints you put on the young women you abducted. Life behind bars is a far cry from what those women go through every day."

She pauses for a moment before speaking. "I know you think that these girls have horrible lives. And, if they stayed in the lives they were in? A frivolous existence of privilege without passion, where appearance matters more than who the person is? Maybe we did them a favor." She shrugs.

"We? Don't want to take responsibility for

the work *you* did Ava? As I understand it, when it came to calling the shots, you were a one-woman operation.

"And am I to assume you didn't come from privilege?" I add. "Well, I did, and one thing privilege gives you is the freedom to choose the life you want."

She shuts down. I can feel it. Well done, Justine. Where's Frankl when I need him.

Silence, and then I break my own cardinal rule and speak first. "You know, Ava, maybe I should ask you if *you* have any questions?"

"What did you study?" she surprises me by asking. I have no idea what "Rachel" studied. Social work comes to mind.

"Actually, I have a PhD in criminal psychology, but I started my career in social work. I got my PhD after working with incarcerated people. That experience pointed out to me that a criminal might be no different from me, but instead had a different origin that set him or her on a predetermined path.

"How about you?" I ask. "What's your background?"

"Are you asking what I was born into, *Doctor*?" she says with a smirk, or is it sarcasm?

"Actually, I think you weren't born into poverty, but maybe middle – mundane, boring – middle class and I think you might have gotten into this in the beginning because risk excites you. And then at some point there was no turning back?"
Shut up Justine.

"Well, aren't you smart. I guess they haven't figured out where I come from yet, huh?"

"Your history, if they know it, is not in the file they gave me. But this is the FBI, it might not be. They tend to leave things out for people like me."
I want her to think I'm not FBI. I laugh to myself. That should be easy, because I'm not FBI.

"Well, Rachel, if that is your real name, where I come from isn't important and it won't provide you anything. *I* won't provide you anything. If I did, I'd be a dead girl before dawn. Because one thing you can be sure of is there are no secrets in the world in which I play, or played, and your people are not part of my cheering squad either."

I don't want to be distracted, but it scares me because I have to depend on the security of the group around me. But I know she's right.

"So, the girls, Ava? How does it work?"

"It works the same way it works in the military. Push pull. Pain pleasure. Break down build up. There's no special technique, but some respond faster than others. That's all. I sometimes wondered why that is, but I never came up with a theory. That's just how it works.

"And we didn't know the girls before we picked them up. It was about how they looked and if we could safely extract them. Nothing more. I assume you know I'm telling the truth, and that is all I'm going to tell you today. What do I get?"

"What do you want?"

"What do you have to offer?"

"I don't know yet," I reply honestly, "but I will see you again and I will have an answer for you. One more thing. The people you dealt with in the Middle East? How did you find them? Did you manipulate them, or just do straight business? What do you think of them?"

She stops and looks at me across the table.

"I was told you were here to give me a psychological evaluation to determine if I'm sane. I think we can drop that ruse. Why are you here, *Doctor*?"

"We need to try and undo some of what you did. Maybe try to save some of them if we can find them. We think you might know where they are. I'm in charge of seeing if you will help us. And I'm in charge of evaluating you. You have a life experience that we rarely find."

"And what do you think?"

"I think you could provide us with invaluable information but I'm not sure I trust you."

She looks at me and doesn't say anything.

I think about the fact that she surely has no idea I'm here as a representative of one of the families from which she stole a child. I assume she thinks I'm government. That works for me.

"We have someone who might go in and meet with the connections we have uncovered from your computer and our intel. We need to find a reason to go in. I want you to give me that."

She looks at me and doesn't say anything. But I think she is thinking about it. I think she did not expect this conversation. Neither did I.

"Anything you can give me could help," I add. I try hard to not sound like I'm desperate, or worse, begging.

She pauses for a moment. "There are two girls that are supposed to be delivered in a few weeks. They are late. I assume you have those girls. That is your bargaining tool. Tell them you are coming to make that drop and they will not want to risk losing their money, or the possibility of getting the girls. That's all I have for you."

"Thank you. It's something. I will find out what I can do for you in return."

She looks at me and I have no idea what she's thinking. I know we are finished. I get up to leave.

"If I make it back, I'll see you again."

I knock on the door to let the guard know I'm finished and leave without looking back.

An hour later I'm back on the plane and the only thing I know is that I will not tell them what I told her. I hope the earrings were just earrings.

CHAPTER SIXTEEN

You're Playing Differently

Later that afternoon, Robert and I are meeting and Coleman is there as well. Coleman wanted me to tell him what happened as soon as I boarded the plane, but I wanted to think through it all and get my story straight. I also didn't want him texting Robert anything about what he thought without telling me. I know I'm less malleable, but I don't understand it all yet. I'm on new ground, which never feels secure.

One thing I know for sure is that I need to determine the narrative around the things I can control. Not give it to others to present and put their twist on when they relay it to Robert. I need to build a layer between him and the team around what I'm experiencing. He needs to hear it from me first.

I can't help but think that my whole life, in business and personally, I've often given it away to someone else to carry, own, or even call theirs. Those days are over, starting now.

When I wasn't saying much about the meeting, Thomas wanted to learn more about me personally on the flight back and something held me back on that as well.

"How did you meet Robert?" he'd asked.

I had no choice but to answer. "Robert and my ex-husband worked together and Robert's ex-wife is my closest friend. Robert and I stayed friends and she remained friends with my ex so the kids could be together no matter who had them. It works for our families." I shut my eyes after that to stop any further questions.

At the meeting I tell Robert and Thomas the bare minimum. I explain what the two criteria are for choosing the women. I tell them I told Ava I would be back and I need to offer her something if I do go back. I don't mention her statement about no one being trustworthy inside our team either, even though she didn't realize what my team entailed. I don't tell them that she didn't repel me, which surprised me. I don't tell them that I want to go back and hear more from her. I have a moment wondering if Coleman wasn't here, would I have said more to Robert?

I'm with them when the text comes in from Tariq.

> *Yes to your idea. Tell me when you are coming back. We will set it up.*

Robert says two days. I text a few days and that I will follow up later when I have the details.

Robert wants to play backgammon before I head home. Tomorrow will be a full day of prepping with the new additions to the team. I haven't seen the disciples since I angered at least some of them and Robert removed me from the room. I'm tired and don't want to play.

"Sure. Let's play ten games and then I'm going home."

I'm a quick backgammon player. I don't always take the time to study the options, and I don't always assess my position on the board long enough before moving. What will happen next? Could I bury my opponent on my next move? Should I use the cube now when he might still take it? Which is the checker least likely to be hit? What is the pip count and who has the advantage around it?

Years of playing have me on a set pattern of visualizing the moves, but leaning on that and not the other considerations means I miss things. Opportunities. Possible setbacks. But, like my newfound thoughtful approach to this mission, I'm slower to move today. I'm considering more than the initial move before committing. Robert notices.

"You're playing differently."

"Am I?"

"Yes, and you know you are."

"Yes, I do." I smile at him and walk away two hours later feeling great about the way I played. When I took the extra time, I saw things I would have overlooked. And by not allowing him to keep the pace quick, which his remarkable mind can do without error, he loses that advantage. I don't have to always allow another to determine the pace of our interactions. Interesting.

CHAPTER SEVENTEEN

Women at the Table

I love having women at the table. The dynamic changes. Maybe because the topic of men enslaving women for their own sexual pleasure makes them a little ashamed of their gender in front of additional women. They seem, well, just a wee bit humbled. But not.

I wish I could articulate it for my own information, but whatever the new dynamic is, it works for me, and I can see immediately it doesn't work as well for them.

The women they brought in are smart, knowledgeable, well-spoken and anyone would have to see they are adding value. There is something else, though. All of a sudden, I find my sense of humor. Not ha ha humor but injecting a line or two that lightens the load, at least for me. The room is lighter.

The psychiatrist who works with trafficked women from the Middle East starts. Her name is Elizabeth and she is behind large glasses and a long-sleeved shirt and scarf so not much of her is exposed. Literally and figuratively. She is a serious person and I wonder what her backstory is. "It's important to understand the difference in the dynamics between a woman chained to a bed to be sexually assaulted by strangers paying for access, and women who have been cultivated to be with a man as if it were a choice.

"It's not, but sometimes the women can lose a sense of reality. Especially once fear recedes to resignation. And it becomes cemented in their psyche when they realize and are grateful that their routine, as bad as it is, no longer has a risk of death. With the dissipation of total fear, they can grow to accept and even find a kind of peace in their new situation.

"It's built on the sands of an inner voice that is protecting them; not giving them a true sense of where they are and what they are experiencing, but it allows them to feel safe and relatively unafraid."

She looks up and waits for some response. There is none.

I learn that in Eastern Europe and Russia there are three kinds of trafficked women: those who thought they were being placed to do domestic work and would be paid and could start a new life; those who were prostitutes and thought they could do better, get paid better and start a new life; and those who thought they were being sent to marry a man who wanted a bride.

All arrive to one of the following scenarios: chained to a bed without any future whatsoever; those who were never paid because they were "paying off the debt of being brought here" and would likely never pay it off; and those who were under the thumb of a pimp they were dependent upon. The bulk of trafficked women have this experience.

And then there are the women tailored to meet the needs of the rich men of the Middle East and some of the power brokers in other countries like Russia, where corruption has left the door open for those who can pay outrageous sums for doing outrageous things.

I learn that these networks could not exist without a corrupt government either looking away, receiving compensation, or participating.

I keep trying to learn what happens inside the heads of the women sold to the elite, for in some cases millions of dollars, and I can't seem to get the answer. Finally I ask, "Is the reason you don't know how these girls get through this trauma because they are rarely, if ever, rescued? You seem to understand how it works with the other trafficked types."

Julia, who hasn't spoken after the introductions, answers. She was trafficked in a way somewhere between being tied to the post and being a high-end prostitute who had amazing clothes from a pimp who still called the shots for her.

She is a doctor now specializing in helping women move on, but as she made clear, not completely recover. Although she is a rare example, she says returning to their former "normal" is not a goal that's attainable. "Recovery and possibility" is the way she describes it.

"We probably don't know much because the girls you will meet come from rich families who take control of their re-entry through private channels and we rarely get access," Julia replies. "They are not part of the system of supports that we have in place. And there are not that many in comparison to the other types. The numbers of those who are trafficked this way are minuscule compared to the other three."

We then move to the goal of the operation I'm about to undertake.

Robert makes it clear, "Justine is on a mission to get information. Where are they? How many? Is there access? Any piece of information you can give Justine will be helpful. What we do with it will be determined after we finish analyzing it. She is not there to take any action. She is just there to gather. At least for now."

"Damn," I say, "I want to be a hunter like all of you."

The other women in the room laugh.

CHAPTER EIGHTEEN

My Posse

It's a day and a half later, and I arrive at the plane and walk on to find Thomas sitting there.

"What are you doing here?" I ask.

"Robert and I thought it would be beneficial for me to work with you on the way over and possibly spend some time strategizing how you will get through these next few days. We can bring him in by phone after we have talked."

"You can't be on the plane when I land in Riyadh."

"You will drop me off in London and pick me up on the way back."

Interesting. No one asked me what I thought of this plan. Last thing I need is to add another three hours to my flights over there and back. I'm tired, and I can't get my friend David's words out of my mind, "Coleman is about the money," he had commented when we discussed Thomas' role on the team. "He's a hired gun. Remember that."

The plane takes off and I purposely sit away from Thomas.

Rich walks back to speak to me about London and how I want to handle things when we land. I look at him and wonder if he thinks it's odd that a military strategist known by nearly every American is on my plane, when I'm supposed to be a consultant for rich people.

He heads back to the cockpit. Wait. This is too much of a coincidence. This trip was planned less than 24 hours ago and both pilots just happen to be available? And there are only two of them, and they will be on call for the next 48 hours at least, which is certainly against FAA regulations, right? Should be a second crew.

I realize I'm the idiot who doesn't get it.

Is it that I'm just not paying attention to what's behind what's in front of me? I've never needed to before now.

The pilots are part of the team. They've known all along.

I walk over and sit next to Thomas.

"Okay. Rich is one of the team, right? He's not a pilot for the leasing company who owns the plane. We own the plane, right?"

He doesn't hesitate. "Yes."

"Why the hell didn't I know that?"

"Because you said you didn't want to know the details."

I don't ever remember saying that, although a week ago it was probably true. Either way, seems like a pretty important detail. "Well, I've changed my mind. Now I want to know them."

"Good girl."

And, don't call me "girl" is what I want to add, but don't. Becoming Clarice will take time.

I take a moment to regroup then walk to the cockpit and ask Rich to come back and speak with me. He says he'll be out in a few minutes. I go back to my seat and try to see him in this new light.

The man is in his late forties and strong but not muscle-bound. He is maybe 5 foot 11 with that kind of brown-haired, brown-eyed face that is pleasant enough but without notable features. He is always looking intently, or so it seems, but in the daylight there are usually aviator sunglasses so it's hard to tell.

He doesn't smile often, but when he does it takes over his face. What I found most compelling about him on the past trips was the way he listened, cocking his head as if he were deciphering the information on multiple levels, which I now realize he was.

I'm glad he knows what's going on. I feel like I have someone I can count on alongside me, especially in the dead of night over the Atlantic Ocean, which is a lonely place. I realize I like him. I find him attractive.

I remember on the first trip when Chip told both pilots to do whatever I said. I told them I don't want anybody giving orders I don't know about. They said "yes, ma'am" and I believed them. Still do.

Rich walks back down the aisle, weaving a bit because of some turbulence, but with the surety of someone who has been here many times and can navigate a little disturbance. He sits down across from me. He fastens his seat belt which shows how he approaches everything. Thorough. Yes, the man is thorough.

We spend the next half hour talking more openly, now that he knows that I know. He seems relieved but doesn't share any personal opinions about anything. He just gives me more information about his background and how he approaches all of this. He was a Navy SEAL and later a pilot.

I ask him about his actual role in the operation. "My job is to take you wherever you ask me to take you, and to not leave until you are safely on the plane. That's my job. Where you go, I go."

"What if I don't come back to the plane?"

"Neither do I. I will find you."

"You don't know me. What if I'm a screw up?"

"I already know you're not. But I'm glad you know we're on the same path here. It helps. I know it must be hard for you to go in alone. I have your back."

I actually believe he does. And, for some reason at that moment I know Coleman doesn't. Funny how when you start to ask yourself who is who and what they are at their core, you find that the heights they've reached might not be what makes them great.

Rich goes back to the cockpit and I feel so much better, stronger. I feel like I'm creating my own posse.

I walk over and sit next to Thomas at the table. We start talking, which continues most of the way to London. He is more than helpful. He talks to me about what to look for. How to assess what

I'm saying and how it's being received on the other side. What things people do when they're lying. He reminds me that the culture I'm going into is alien to me and from what he knows of me thus far, against my nature.

He talks to me about the men in power in Saudi Arabia and gives me information about their backgrounds and why they feel the way they do. He describes Middle Eastern men and their attitudes regarding women and sex. "They take what they want from women, and they believe it is their right to take what they want. That women are property. Baby makers. Homemakers. They treat their wives well, but any other class of women is fair game."

He is mesmerizing and has this smooth way of talking and touching my arm that isn't sexual, but is validating, and it feels comforting in a way.

I sleep. He sleeps. We land in London to drop him off and then take off almost immediately, arriving in Riyadh in the early morning. I go to the Four Seasons Riyadh, check in and crash for a few hours.

I wake up and text Tariq that I'm here and waiting for instructions. He texts me back that I will be picked up at 11 p.m. this evening, which seems odd. Why so late?

I turn on CNN, rest and eat dinner in my room, waiting for 11 p.m. I'm getting anxious so I try to meditate, which is not my natural state. Yet another tool in my toolbox. When Dry was working with me on how to get into a meditative state, she told me to start with just a few minutes. I will get better in time. Not sure that's true, but I want to be cool and clear and calm and calculating.

CHAPTER NINETEEN

Night Visit

I'm in the back of the car. I'm wearing a
burka. I like that. Hide in plain sight. The windows
are darkly tinted and we've been on the road for an
hour, but I'm not sure if we are driving in circles or
going to one place. Lots of turns. I'm surprised and
nervous that Tariq isn't in the car. Just the driver.
He doesn't say a word. Neither do I.

We pull up to a compound surrounded by an
eight-foot stucco wall. A man walks out, opens the
door and ushers me into a hallway with terracotta
floors and four hallways leading off the entrance.
Another man, dressed in a dark Western suit
emerges from one of the hallways, walks over to me
and with a Saudi accent says, "Follow me, please."

We head back down the hallway he came from and then through another hallway, and into a room which is gold and white, lush but understated; not steeped in that gaudy gild that I associate with immense wealth in the Middle East.

The lighting is subdued and there are some fragrant candles lit on a table. The scent is not familiar but so calming. I love the room. It's larger than a normal living room, but not so large as to feel cavernous. Actually, I could live in this room. I've never seen one quite like it.

There is a woman seated on the couch and she motions for me to sit next to her. She is wearing a burka as well, and as soon as my guide leaves and shuts the door she removes it. Her hair is light brown with golden tints and when she turns to me, I'm stunned.

"Hello Ms. Lloyd, I'm Sakirah and I will be helping you understand what the challenges are here, with the hope that you will have some ideas that will help make sure that everything is being done for the women's comfort."

I can't respond. I keep looking to make sure. The woman is Caroline. I'm sure of it. She looks like the picture Robert showed me, but older. Colder? I still can't speak. But I know I need to say something to make sure she doesn't sense something is wrong.

I look away and remove my burka.

"I think this is the most serene room I've ever been in. It's beautiful."

"It's one of my rooms and I thought it would be more comfortable to meet here. I'm glad you feel at home."

"Your English is perfect."

"Does that surprise you?"

"No, but I haven't been in this country long and you are the first woman I've met. The men all have accents. It stands out to me." I have no idea where I'm going.

A young woman, covered from head to foot comes in and puts tea and some sort of pastry down on the table and quietly leaves. Caroline speaks to her in what can only be perfect Arabic, and the women nods yes as she exits.

"Do you know Tariq?" I ask.

"No."

"He is my contact," I tell her. "And he has told me that some of the women my network has provided are having difficulties. We thought perhaps if I could meet with them or hear what is going on I might be able to provide some help.

She doesn't say anything and then quietly says, "Some of the women are becoming inwardly focused, not communicating with other women. We don't know why or how to help them. They are depressed."

I have to ask. "Were you brought in the way they were?"

"No. I am married. But I care about them and I've been allowed to help them adjust after they arrive here."

That's it. That's all she says. I wonder at her poise, her surety, and no sign of the victim I know she is.

"Can I meet some of the women and maybe we can speak with them before I make my recommendations? I'd like to hear what they have to say."

"Next time maybe. I haven't set it up but can look into it," she pauses, "if we move forward."

I can tell she's not sure what I'm offering and neither am I. I get the feeling she feels she is in the power position of deciding what my exposure will be. Is she?

"I think that if I can see how they're living I can help assess how we might move forward and even perhaps make some changes in my own program to make it all work better."

"I think we can do that," she says.

Everything she is saying is keeping me off balance. I realize I haven't pulled myself together since our introduction.

She continues, "I can arrange for you to come back and I can show you around and you can meet some of the women."

"Yes," I say. "I can do that and I think it will be helpful."

I look around and wonder if there is a microphone; if we are truly in a private setting or if someone is watching or listening. I need to decide what to do next. My fear is that I might never see her again.

I take out paper and a pen from my bag. I write Robert's name on the paper and my cell phone number.

"Here is my number if you want to contact me directly. Could you memorize it please? I never leave a paper with my number anywhere."

She looks at it, studies it, and then hands it back to me. Her expression does not change.

"I don't need your number. I will contact you through the channels you are presently using. Thank you for coming so late."

I rip up the paper into tiny pieces and put it in the candle's flame. I wait until it's burned.

She presses a button under the coffee table and the man comes back to escort me out. It occurs to me that I didn't touch the tea or pastry.

In the car I'm reeling. She looks like she belongs here. She does not look like she's being held against her will or that the last twenty years were the way I assumed they were.

She is lovely, lithe, confident and present. And I'm sure it's her. What I'm not sure about is what to do next. I do know I need to understand more before I tell Robert that I found her. As I think about it, I think he would go in like the Normandy Invasion, and for some reason, I want to see what Caroline does before letting him decide what will happen next.

CHAPTER TWENTY

No Reason for the Holdup

Tariq calls the next morning to tell me I will have another meeting in five days.

"Five days? I don't have five days to wait. Can't you move it up?"

"No," he says.

"I'm going back to the States then," I say.

"I thought you might say that. I need you to take some packages back to the States for me. Someone will pick them up from the airport. I assume you are flying into New York?"

I panic. "Yes, of course."

I text Rich and tell him to get to the plane; that I will be there in a few hours and we will be carrying cargo. Not sure I should say anything else, but I'm nervous. Why are they postponing my next meeting until next week? What am I carrying? Are they following me? I know the flight can't be detected and when I actually fly into Palm Beach, I don't go through any customs or check points; but I don't think I can say no.

I pack up and head to the airport. I board the flight and in the cabin are three large boxes. No notation on them. I don't like it.

Henry does a cursory check with some type of handheld explosive trace detector but I don't know enough about its accuracy to feel totally secure. For every new device, criminals seem to find a workaround.

And bombs aren't the only scary contraband.

But I tell Rich we are good to go.

Minutes pass. Tens of minutes. Rich comes back and looks worried. He says, "I don't have clearance to take off. I'm not sure what is holding us up, but I wanted you to know."

He hands me a piece of paper. Not sure if there are microphones in the boxes?

No reason for the hold up. I don't like it. Will wait a little longer and then get back to you.

I sit there.

An hour goes by. Rich comes back out and

says he can't get an answer. I realize I need to take action and Clarice's voice rises up within me.

"Rich, please tell the tower to call Tariq at this number and tell him I'm being held up. He knows I'm on a tight timeline. Tell them I will call him myself to find out why they're holding us without reason in five minutes if we are not airborne."

I know instantly it is one of three things. Caroline didn't like the whole thing and they uncovered something upon closer scrutiny. They are blowing us up with an explosive in one of the boxes to get rid of "Ava" as no longer serving them. Or there is a customs issue and it's a legitimate holdup. I was told they might come on the flight to check the plane when we landed or before takeoff and that I shouldn't be surprised. Or one other possibility. They are just incompetent.

Two minutes later, Rich comes on the intercom and says we are taking off.

I shut my eyes and can feel the tears rolling down my cheeks. I realize in that moment, as we continue to climb, that there is real risk, danger, in what I'm doing. I realize that even though there are many people involved in this operation, I'm alone over here and that I'm not qualified to be calling the shots.

I text Robert and tell him we will speak in the morning because we don't know whether the boxes are bugged. I tell him we're headed back and won't be stopping in London. Thomas can take a commercial flight home. He texts back that we will meet the following afternoon.

I know not to say anything until the boxes are off the plane after we land. I put my seat back and close my eyes. I keep seeing the plane exploding over the Atlantic from a bomb that is inside one of the boxes. I drift off to a troubled sleep filled with me trying to get away from a box that shows up everywhere I go.

CHAPTER TWENTY-ONE

When You Think of Me

"Hi David," I say from the car on my way to Palm Beach the next afternoon to meet with the team. I haven't filled him in and he left a number of messages for me over the past week.

I realize now that I wish I'd never included him. It seems like such a long, long time ago that I was deciding whether or not to even be a part of this.

"Listen, Justine. I've given this a lot of thought and you have to believe in your own instincts and start to take charge of some of these things they're setting up for you. I'm assuming you're in the thick of it all. You are smart, and you can see what they cannot, and besides, I keep telling you they have a conflict of interest, and your concerns don't necessarily align with theirs.

"They want to keep this going as long as possible so they can get paid as long as possible. They want to impress Robert, and they might not consider your well-being in the process. Promise me you'll think through what's next."

"I promise. I promise." I reassure him. "But to tell you the truth, it's not happening. I'm on the outside now. Don't worry."

I know he doesn't believe me. Fine.

After we hang up, I think about that first day when I arrived just before Robert. I sat at the table trying to look in check, and they ignored me until he arrived. And if I review the meetings since, they never once solicited my opinion based on my experience.

At the time, I wanted them to like me, to not say when I left the room that I was difficult, or aggressive, or anything other than cooperative. Now all I care about is getting Caroline home.

And there's a question I want to answer for myself before I enter the room this time.

I drive by the house and down to the beach. I get out of the car and walk down to sit by the water. I'm not going to leave until I have some clarity about what I want the team to think of when they think of me; words that highlight what I bring to the table.

The words come to me almost immediately: Intuitive. Courageous. Committed. Smart. Yes. Those words ring true and I hope I can live up to them.

My mind wanders to thoughts of Caroline again. Maybe it wasn't her? But it was. What happened to her? What do I say and why am I feeling like I shouldn't say anything yet? How could I not say anything?

Maybe it's because I can't resolve how comfortable I thought she looked. How she appeared to belong there? How could she belong anywhere that was a destination after abduction? Who should I speak to? Dry? Is her obligation to them or to me?

I call Dry's number and she answers.

"Hello Justine."

"Quick question. If I tell you something, are you obligated to report it? What is my privacy limit with you?"

"Anything you say to me goes no further."

"Thanks. I may call you back later."

I get up, stride to the car and head to the house with confidence. I'm not saying anything yet.

Everyone is there. I'm the last to arrive and Robert motions me next to him.

"We read your report. We x-rayed the packages before they picked them up, and it's artifacts. Museum quality. Looks like it was an honest 'can I hitch a ride' by them. So, we don't see any evidence that you're in danger of discovery."

He finishes a few minutes later and one of the men says, "Your report didn't say much about the woman you met with. What did she look like?"

I'm prepared. "She was wearing a burka so I have no idea."

No one seems concerned.

The rest of their conversation is conjecture and my mind wanders back to Caroline. I know I need to get more information.

When the meeting starts to break, I ask Robert to walk with me to the beach. We head to the gate, walk in silence to the ocean and sit down facing the water.

"Robert, what was Caroline like? Was she troubled? Shy? Who was she?"

"I don't know. She did well in school, was attractive and seemed to love her life. I was happy when she was around but I can't say much more. Why?"

I don't respond. I try to find the right way to say what I need to say next. "Robert, the woman I met with was Caroline. I spoke with her. I didn't want you to read it in the report. I just didn't want to put it in front of you without being here in person."

He is silent. It seems like forever.

"What did she say?"

"Not a lot. I don't know if she wasn't sure whether her room was bugged or what, but she seemed calm and collected. She is lovely and put together and well taken care of, but maybe most important, I need to tell you she is not disconnected. She is engaged. And she is a wife to the man who originally purchased her. I don't know anything else.

"We're going to speak again when I go back and I think she will set it up for somewhere outside of the sheik's compound where we met."

"Why did they have you meet her?" he asks.

"I can't say for sure, but I think she has a higher standing than the other women, and for some reason she is maybe friends, or working with them? I don't know for sure. We didn't go there yet.

"Robert, she seemed comfortable in this amazing sitting room that was so simple and beautiful, and when I told her I thought it was one of the nicest rooms I'd ever been in, she thanked me. I can't tell you more than that. She was lovely. Calm and seemingly fine."

I pause waiting to see if he wants to say anything. He isn't looking at me, so I continue. "I need more time with her, but she was totally with me and when I told her you sent me, she looked unfazed. But we were in a room in a large compound, and I have no idea who else was there or listening. I wrote your name on a piece of paper and after she saw it, I burned it. She just took it in and then indicated I should wait until we spoke next."

He still isn't looking at me and I can't help but think that the apple doesn't fall far from the tree because he is as closed as she was. I let the silence sit. I'm content to sit next to him and he doesn't seem as if he's in a hurry to move on. He just sits.

"What does she look like?"

"Exactly like the girl in the picture, but older. Not worn, just older. And she still has the clear gaze I saw in the picture. I know she can't be the same person, Robert, but she is not destroyed. I promise you that."

He looks at me for the first time, and he looks different. I'm not sure how. He doesn't hold my gaze long enough to have me see more, but I feel even looking me in the eye is his thank you. I'm not going to get more and it's enough. More than enough. I sense he is done talking to me and needs time for himself.

I stand up.

"I will see you tomorrow, Robert. Please let me know when and who you tell about Caroline, and if this changes anything. I think I have to let her determine what happens next, and unless she betrays me, I want to trust her with the information I gave her.

"I think we should hold off on a set plan until I see her next. The fact that Tariq is saying I should come back in five days means something is going on. If I'm wrong, then I'm okay with that too. I want to get her what she needs if she needs anything."

I lean down and hug him and walk away. I turn back before heading to the driveway and he hasn't moved a muscle.

When I get home Robert calls on the secure phone. That's a first.

"Thomas wants to meet. Just the three of us. Can you do it tonight for dinner?"

"Yes. I'll see you then."

CHAPTER TWENTY-TWO

Relax, It's Only Dinner

I head over for dinner with Robert and Thomas. I'm fading fast. Bone tired. That deep kind of tired that's ignored when there isn't time to sleep. I wonder about dinner and Coleman's take on the new information about Caroline.

I think about the cocktail party I attended with friends the night before. I left within a half hour. Everyone asking how I was and where I'd been. I felt so disconnected.

How do you express that your entire sense of self is changing; when you can't say why or how or what you feel like standing at some irrelevant cocktail party now? Engaging in conversations about appearances and tennis tournaments you couldn't care less about.

How do you diplomatically say, "I have no interest in your small talk, or your perceived brilliant analysis of what's happening in the world, which to my mind is not brilliant at all?"

Best to leave that aside for now.

The dining room table is set for three, but neither of them has arrived yet. I can hear people talking outside and realize that the weekend guests are going to eat out there while we eat inside. I wonder if they are at cocktails.

I walk over and look at a Rothko hanging at the end of the room. I like Rothko. I've seen many of them in many different environments, Harvard's mess hall housing one of my favorites. But Rothkos unprotected fade, and the Harvard Rothko suffers from lack of protection. I'm always in wonder of how it fits everywhere, and nowhere. Maybe that will be me after this is over.

Thomas comes in first and gives me a hug. It's the first time I notice that he hugs just a little too long, too familiar.

"How are you? Wow. What a development. You are doing great! I'm proud of you."

Proud of me? Not sure you get to take pride of ownership for my work. I always hated that my mother took my accomplishments and made the genesis of them her. When someone says to me, "You should be so proud of Michael's achievements," I always respond, "They aren't mine, they're all his."

"I'm good Thomas. How about you?"

He laughs. "Well, you left me stranded in London and taking a commercial flight home, but other than that, I'm good."

I don't see any point in replying.

"Do you like Rothko?" I ask instead, nodding toward the painting.

"Is it a Rothko? I wouldn't know a Rothko from a Picasso."

"Well, I wouldn't know a portrait of one colonel from another, so we're even."

"I remember sitting for my portrait at the Pentagon," he says. "Waste of time."

"Yes, it is actually. All you men wearing silly Halloween costumes if you ask me. And the shiny medals? Seriously? What's the point of them?"

He looks at me. "The point of them is power and exhibiting it to those who need to follow you."

"Interesting."

Robert walks in and sits down next to Thomas at one side of the table. He motions for me to sit across from them and I notice that there is no head of the table. I read somewhere that sitting across from someone at a table sets up an automatic barrier between people. I guess we'll see.

A salad comes out and Robert asks them to shut the door on the way out. I know the room is swept often and that it is clean, but I'm still nervous with so many people around outside.

"Thomas met with me after our meeting today," Robert begins. "He has some ideas about next steps before we let the team know about Caroline." He says her name naturally now, and that feels different.

I start to cut up my garden salad with pears and a drizzle of some sort. Might be raspberry. It's delicious.

Thomas waits until I look up from chewing. I set my fork down.

He says, "I can see you are starting to think through things in a strategic way. Good for you. I welcome that."

You welcome that? I say nothing.

"I'd like to think that part of the way you are looking at things comes from our time together sorting through what operations like this face and how to approach them."

You think wrong, my friend.

"Anyway, I'm concerned about your meeting and taking the next meetings by yourself. Especially because we're uncertain whose side she's on yet. I think it puts you at a disadvantage."

I'm listening. I look up and say, "What do you suggest to offset what you see as a weakness?"

"I think we send one of the team in with you. Obviously one of the women. This also allows us another option if you need to remove yourself. You can introduce her as your number one associate."

Wow.

I look at Robert, raise my eyebrows, and take another bite of the salad. I also reach for the bread, lest anyone think I'm disturbed by this in the least.

Robert says, "I don't know what to think. Thomas walked me through some of what you two went over on the plane and how he prepped you for the last meeting. It seems a lot of what you came to was planted in that meeting on the plane."

"I need to marinate in this for a few minutes," I say. "I'm going to finish my salad. You talk amongst yourselves while I think through what is being proposed."

They start eating their salads, but I know that Thomas knows what I think.

I simmer but manage to put in a few light remarks during the rest of the course. Robert pushes the button to remove the salads and the next course of shrimp risotto arrives. My sister's recipe for risotto from her book, *Relax, It's Only Dinner,* is the best risotto in the land. Relax, it's only dinner.

I respond to Coleman's earlier remarks, "I have a few things to say. I appreciated your help in teaching me how to assess things, Thomas. It was truly invaluable. The signs you gave me for determining truth versus lies and whether they like me or are just pretending gave me the confidence to believe in the way I was presenting myself. And that gave me room to assess what everyone's been saying.

"So, I'll credit you with the assist on it all. I don't want to belabor who got us where on this. I think it's much more important to determine what moves the project forward successfully and keeping Caroline safe and visible to us. I'm sure if we don't handle this well, the odds of ever finding her again go south, and let's be real, we don't know who she was sold to and exactly where she is. I don't agree that I'm getting in over my depth now, which is the only reason you would want to make this change.

"I am in. They think I'm Ava. Caroline didn't

reject what I put in front of her. So far, I'm moving the operation forward as planned. Why risk it? There hasn't been another person introduced by Ava as her assistant, and I think it would be an alarm bell that could shut the whole thing down.

"I'm not having trouble with anything so far, and while I realize it might get much tougher, I can safely say that I think we should not do anything, and I mean *anything* to give them a moment's pause. The real risk here is to me, not to Caroline. When I'm there, I have zero power over her.

"The only reason to do what you suggest is if the agent, me, is failing. I'm not. I vote no. I do want this to be over as soon as possible. But I think your plan extends it or even puts it at risk. So, no. I'm a no-go on this."

Thomas smiles but he had taught me what to look for and he doesn't meet my eyes and I definitely see his face tense.

I take another bite.

I look at Robert and smile.

"Robert, you said you thought I was the right person for this job. I now think you were right. I'm non-threatening. I think well on my feet and I have good instincts. And I think adding another person now is a mistake. A big mistake.

"After twenty-five years of looking for her, are you willing to risk it? Let's be honest. The worst-case scenario is I disappear. And I can honestly say I will take that risk for what I consider a larger reward possibility.

"But set all that aside. Again, Ava has worked with these people for years and from what we can tell, never brought another person in. All of a sudden she shows up with someone? Why? To what end for Ava? I don't think it holds up to scrutiny and that should be the real driving factor to whether we add a person on my team or not."

He waits two minutes before answering. Robert is never afraid of silence. I have always admired that in him. I still the ten other things I want to spew out to make my case. I don't need to justify my position.

"Thomas, I think she's right. Let's stick with the plan, but why don't you fly over with her again next week and prep again."

Believe it or not he says, "Yes, sir."

I can only think that you can take the man out of the armed forces but you can't take the armed forces out of the man.

"Robert, let's play some backgammon after dinner, okay? I need a break from this."

I look pointedly at Coleman. I have years and years with Robert. I am not some pretty pawn you can direct in your micro war here. Don't fuck with me.

CHAPTER TWENTY-THREE

The Doubling Cube

I walk into the Mothership and it's clear they
have been meeting for quite some time. There
are empty bottles of water scattered throughout.
Everyone looks tired. And when I arrive, the
conversation that was in full force stops.

I sit next to Julia and look at her. She shrugs.

Robert speaks first.

"We are thinking about how to follow you in
and extract Caroline when you meet with her. The
team feels that's what she is setting up during this
week; why she seemed to want to let you know you
would meet her elsewhere."

WTF? I say nothing. I'm not sure how to
approach what I think is a terrible, terrible mistake.

"Robert I might not have been clear. I surmised she wanted to meet elsewhere, and that maybe it wasn't safe to speak in her personal living room, but she didn't say that. Our meeting was over a few minutes after I showed her my note with your name on it. She definitely had no time to put anything together. I think she wanted to think about it all.

"And I don't think for one minute this plan is anything other than nuts. She should have a say. What if there are children? What if there is more going on? Additional people she wants out? This is not just about her at this point. You have to let me have more time with her. At least one more meeting."

It's not lost on me that it took him twenty-five years to find her. He isn't going to let someone take her underground for another twenty-five. He doesn't care about anything or anyone else.

There are too many people in here. Way too many people.

I look at Thomas and send him a text.

Get everyone out of here. They want a rescue mission. It's in their sweet spot and Robert isn't thinking clearly. You, me and Robert should go over this!

He looks at my text, saying nothing. I start to panic.

A minute or so later when there is a lull, he says, "Everyone take a break. Justine, Robert and I will take it from here."

They all walk out, Jason turns back as he's leaving and says, "If she is suffering from Stockholm Syndrome, this is the only chance we'll have. Remember that."

I look at Robert and I can tell he's exhausted. I look at Coleman and wonder if he's the one who left me out of the meeting until now. It's not about me, I remind myself and concentrate on what Coleman is saying.

"Robert," Coleman says gently, "if this were my daughter, I'd already be in there guns blazing. And I would be wrong. Justine is right. We cannot plan for this properly because Justine will have no idea where she is going or what the plan is until she's in the car. We do not have safe access to this geo area. We do not have a team that has practiced and worked together planning the extraction. We have no idea where this meeting is going to take place so we cannot plan to extract safely.

"Caroline could, actually most likely *would*, be killed. Justine's cover would be blown immediately and she would be killed. Or perhaps worse, they both could disappear and I promise you this would be over.

"Justine needs to go back in and find out what Caroline wants. She needs to find out what Caroline thinks. She needs to find out more about the network and how it works. It's way too early to bring this to a climax. You must trust me on this."

Robert gets up slowly. "You are right. You run the plan. I'm going to step aside for now. Justine, come and see me when you're done. I'll be in the library."

He leaves. Coleman brings the team back in and starts to set up the plan. Lots of pushback. I tune out.

An hour later, I leave and walk to the library. I realize that Thomas is in charge now.

I approach Robert, "Hi. You okay?"

"Yes, what's the plan?" he says.

"I go in and find out what she wants and then we regroup."

"Okay."

"Robert, I think you and I should meet with Dr. Ryan to talk about what Caroline might have gone through and how best to work with her. But I think I go down to D.C. first and meet with Ava to see what she can tell me about Caroline, or maybe we should start referring to her as Sakirah. I think that will help us. I know we don't trust Ava totally but I think I'd like to speak to her about Sakirah.

"Then you and I meet with Dry and take it from there. I don't think the entire team needs to know all this and you can tell them what you want them to know on a need-to-know basis."

"Yes, I like it. Yes." But he looks so tired.

"Want to play backgammon?"

He looks up at me. "Yes."

We play without speaking for the next four hours. We both get more than a second wind. We are flying. The dice are flying. They bring us sandwiches and Diet Coke and we don't even look up. The thing about backgammon is you have to focus on it totally, and yet you can play it by rote. But you will never play it well if you don't consider all the options.

I have never doubled more. Neither has he. In one game the cube goes to 32, which I've never seen in a match I've been in before. I reflect later on the fact that the doubling cube, which is about doubling the amount you are risking on that one game, is key to winning a match, or losing one. And assessing the risk before turning the cube over to your opponent or accepting the cube, is the decision that could win or lose you the entire match.

It's just like life I realize. And Robert is seeing the cube turning every time a decision needs to be made. And this decision might just determine whether or not his twenty-five-year search comes to a positive end. Or not.

And so we play on. Cubing more than we ever have, but it still isn't out of control. He actually wins, and I'm good with it because I know I've never played better. I sleep like a baby when I get home.

CHAPTER TWENTY-FOUR

They Will Betray You

Ava walks in, sits down, and looks at me.

"You look different," she says.

"I'm tired? I'm wiser? I don't know. But frankly, you look different too. Are you okay? You look, I don't know, softer."

"Maybe resigned is the right word for me. Finished? I don't know either."

We both pause, not able to continue to another level of relationship, but wanting to acknowledge the other's point of view. This is so strange.

"I met a woman I think you might have placed. She goes by Sakirah. I want you to tell me what you know about her."

After a pause she says, "I would guess that she didn't seem surprised that you were me or give you much information. I don't know much about her other than she's the gem of Sheik Habil's women and she is now a wife to him. I had never known that to happen, ever. I think she's smart and played him, and maybe still does, but I don't know anything other than that."

"Did you know her when she first got there?" I ask.

"Yes, she was one of mine."

I try to not show my surprise. Shock. Wait, supposedly Ava has only been doing this for fifteen years. This makes her lying about it, but I know I can't ask because then she will know that I know more about Caroline than she thinks.

"What was she like?"

"She was memorable. She was calm. Don't get me wrong, she was terrified, but she didn't react with the stages we are used to. Fighting like a crazy person. Breaking down over and over again with tears and pleas. She just glazed over.

"It's hard to remember it all but she was memorable because she was different and maybe that's why she rose the way she did. I can't tell you how out of character it is that she could become a wife, but she was also lucky. He hasn't bought a lot of women and has a smaller group than others with less resources than he has. She got lucky."

"Is it possible he saw in her something that appealed to him and it wasn't random?" I ask.

"No actually, that's not possible. They only see them on a tape and she was drugged and he would not have known what she was like. No, it's not possible."

Luck of the draw. I think of backgammon, and how luck plays an element in it where other games like chess do not. Twenty-two percent luck. And it means that someone who is much better than you can lose to you. And vice versa. And I think that maybe even though she was drugged, he saw something in her glance at the camera. I also realize that I hope that tape is long gone. That no one ever gets to see Caroline exposed that way in the FBI investigation.

"What happens to those tapes?"

"They are destroyed," she replies. "I personally destroy them. But the person who purchases the girl has a copy. I have no idea what they do with theirs."

"So, what do you know about where Sakirah came from before she was picked up?"

"I don't remember but I think her dad was a successful Wall Street guy and she was from a private school in New York City. But I don't remember much else. There was a huge media blitz when she was taken, but she was long gone. Someone like that who is picked up outside the United States is never recovered.

"Usually we have a few days before they realize she's gone and that gives us time to get away without leaving much of a trace. Sometimes, and I can't remember if it was true with her, we have days before anyone knows she is missing."

Brearley. She was from Brearley and had just finished. She was headed to Princeton in the fall, you bitch.

"What about her friend that she was traveling with? What happened to her?"

"I never told you she was with someone."

Shit.

"Well, you said you picked her up in Europe, so I can't believe she was alone. And, you said you had a few days lead, so she wasn't in a group."

"No, I didn't say that. I said *sometimes* we have a few days lead and I didn't remember."

She looks at me pointedly. I think she wants me to know that she knows there is more going on here than me being an agent trying to take down the network. I wonder if I've shown too much interest in Caroline and have not asked more questions overall.

Either way, I have to believe it won't matter in the end. That those who are handling her are all working on the side of justice. But I also note that the FBI people think I'm a psychiatrist and I get nervous.

"Ava, why did you do this? I haven't seen your personal history in the file. I know that you're from a poor family in New York City but went to Kent on a full scholarship and then the University of Michigan with a full ride. What happened to you?"

"Nothing. I wanted money. I found my way into it and grew my business. The motivation was money," she says with little affect.

"Really? Interesting considering the way you've lived. Middle class all the way including your food and clothing. Tons of money in accounts overseas, but you never spent any of it. So, money motivated you?"

I want her to know that I see through her the same way she sees through me. "I think I'm done here. Is there anything you want to say?" I ask.

"Don't think you can lure these people into

your web to destroy the network," she warns. "They will betray you." She says it with almost a proud association, but I can't help but think she doesn't necessarily want to see me destroyed either. Not sure where the feeling comes from, but on a visceral level I know she's trying to warn me for my own good.

As I walk to the car and all the way back on the flight, I think about how I can figure out what Caroline wants. Or if what she is going to tell me she wants, is what she truly wants. Or, if she has already betrayed me.

CHAPTER TWENTY-FIVE

Lessons from Elizabeth Smart

As I'm filling Robert in on my meeting with Ava, he leans forward taking in every word. He responds in a way that is different. Almost responding as if he can't hold it back; not measured, and well after the fact. I'm thrilled it's just the two of us.

"We thought at first they were taken in Paris, but we now believe they were taken in Rome," says Robert. "Right after they arrived. It was a nightmare because there were no leads. And, five years ago, when I brought Coleman in, he changed how we approached it all. He started at the other end. Where they would have ended up, and we knew it was either Moscow or the Middle East.

And back then it would have been Saudi Arabia. Dubai wasn't even an option. And that's how we figured it out. Backtracking from where they would have been delivered."

"Do you know what happened to her friend? What is her name?"

"Her name is Sophie. Her family didn't want to work together. We have watched over the years and I think they moved on. Got divorced. It broke them. And it broke Caroline's mother. They called it an accidental overdose, but she killed herself a year later. I didn't think Caroline should go on the trip, and she did." He stops talking and I wonder if it became the blame game. And I wonder if Caroline knows.

The computer screen lights up and Dry's face is on the screen and we face the screen and I open with, "Hello Dr. Ryan, do you know Robert Bradbury?"

"Yes."

"We want to speak with you about Caroline. I've gone over with Robert what happened when I met her and what Ava said. We are looking for some insight as to what Caroline went through after she was taken; and what I can do to assess her authenticity when I go back tomorrow. What I can do to help her if that is needed. Actually, we aren't sure what we want. We just want you to tell us what you think."

"I haven't met her, or seen her reactions to you on tape, so I can't speak to who she is now," Dr. Ryan advises. "But I can give you some examples that might help you decipher what's going on."

Robert nods.

"Every single girl or woman who goes through this handles it differently. Patty Hearst had to go to jail. To this day she is surrounded by bodyguards and she married one, but she has also gone on to create a seemingly stable environment for her children.

"Most likely, even with the therapy she received which was substantial during and after her prison term, she never went through what you need to go through to truly gain some ground toward recovery, which is never complete. She lives on the surface. So, she appears to cope, and she does, but the price she pays keeps her isolated from those around her because they will never understand what happened to her and neither does she.

"Then you have someone like Elizabeth Smart," Dry continues. "You remember her. The Mormon girl abducted from her bed in the middle of the night in Salt Lake City. Young. Tons of family and community support to help her, and her parents brought in therapists who had the knowledge base to truly help. She also had such a stable homelife beforehand and was able to articulate what happened to her and deal with each aspect of it.

"But her mother also said something interesting to her when she returned. She told her that for nine months she had no control over what happened to her, but now she was in total control over how she let this evil affect her. That Brian David Mitchell had no control over her now and would never again have control.

"She is married now, has children and what tells me she has made real progress is she speaks and is an advocate around dealing with what happened to her for others. That's a good sign, actually. I have not met with or have any inside knowledge of either of these two girls.

"But from what we are learning about Caroline, she has done an incredible job of getting herself in a position to help herself. She seems to be smart and also resilient. I would imagine she was like that most of her life and it's part of her DNA makeup, which judging from your makeup Robert, shouldn't surprise us."

"Can I trust her not to betray me?" I ask.

"No, you can trust her to have thoughtfully planned out what she is going to do next and you are collateral damage if that's what you need to be for her to succeed."

"Well, as far as I can see, that wraps that up. Great. Don't worry about me. I'll be fine." I go with humor. Where else can I go?

Dry smiles and seems to look at me not Robert.

"But you need to remember Justine, you have some of the qualities she does. You are a chameleon and can fit in anywhere and will fit in if you need to in order to survive. You keep your own counsel. You are smart. You are intuitive. She might have met her match in you.

"But you will be on her territory, and she has exit capabilities that you will not have once you get off that plane. But you can't control that part of it, so focus on what you can control. Just like Elizabeth Smart's mother told her to do."

What might that be I wonder?

CHAPTER TWENTY-SIX

Others Had No Agency

David calls me before I head to the plane the next morning. I pick up without wanting to or having anything to share. I no longer need him the way I did at the beginning, and I can see the danger in anyone outside the team knowing anything.

I think about how I used to feel that if I disappeared, David would not let them define the message, and that he would deliver the message to Michael. Actually, I think I'm taking control of who I share my thoughts with and am looking for expertise more than emotional support now.

He asks about Coleman.

"He's not around right now," I lie.

"Don't trust him, Justine."

"He's good at what he does," I reply. "I can trust that. But I hear you. And thanks."

I know I can't totally trust him. David, however, is coming from his own dislike of the man and not assessing Coleman's role in my situation. And his role in my situation is critical and might even be keeping me safe.

I've experienced Coleman taking my point of view and giving it his blessing even when it might not be popular with the team he's assembled. I think that means "getting it right" is his number one priority.

"I have limited personal experience with him, granted," David adds, "but I know he's a hired gun. Do not trust him, Justine. Look, Robert trusts you and he went with your plan, not anyone else's. Don't look back."

I arrive at the plane and Coleman is already on it. He's seated himself on the side couch and has a boatload of papers on the table in front of him. "Come sit with me. I have a lot to go over with you."

I have never liked sitting on the same side of a banquette, even on a date. I like looking across into someone's eyes, not sitting next to them where you have to turn and find their face. But I sit down next to him. The plane takes off and we get started.

He is brilliant. We go through the men who have purchased the girls and what they do in the government and what we know about their psychological makeup. All things considered, Caroline's sheik is nowhere near the top of the evil totem pole. But he *bought* her. It was intriguing and repelling, all at the same time. He was born into a life of wealth and privilege, but he is well-respected and not rowing in a sea of corrupt actions to gain money and power.

Then he asks me about Robert. "How are you finding Robert?"

"How do you mean?"

"Do you think he's holding up? How was the call with Dr. Ryan? I should have been on it."

"I think he's fine. The call with her was short and she was clear about not being able to give us information on Caroline because she hasn't seen or met her."

Note to self, find out why Coleman knows about our meetings that don't include him. See if I can fix that. Robert and I had established between ourselves that Robert would determine what about Caroline would be passed to the team, and Coleman having total access to Robert's schedule doesn't sit well. I doubt Robert mentioned the meeting. I assume Coleman knew because he is given Robert's schedule.

We eat dinner and keep going over background information. Three hours later, I'm tired. He sees my stamina fading.

"I know you must be exhausted. You've flown back and forth through numerous time zones four times in less than two weeks, and the amount of information you've taken in would slay most minds.

"And what you might not yet understand is that when the body goes through the adrenaline rushes of fear and deceit, which have been part of this experience, it takes a toll. Most of us have trouble sleeping and when we do sleep, it's fitful and we don't feel safe, so we sit in a light sleep more often than we should."

"Thanks for saying that," I say. "Hearing it out loud from you makes me feel better. I can't sleep much but when I finally lie down, I feel like I'm going to sleep for twenty-four hours straight."

He nods, "I have to go through these papers and make sure we have everything covered. Lie down and you will probably be able to get some hours in."

He moves a pillow over to me on the seat and pats it. I lie down with my head on the pillow and fall immediately into a deep sleep.

Danger. Danger.

The lights are off in the cabin, the table put away, and Thomas is stroking my head.

"Relax," he says. "I can make you relax. We can do this together. I know I can help you through everything coming up. Just let go and let me relax your body the way it needs right now. Trust me." And then he slips his hand into my shirt from just below my chin and into my bra and starts to stroke my breast. I can't breathe. I can't move.

It takes just a few seconds and then I bolt upright. I'm confused and scared, but alert and ready.

"What the hell are you doing?"

"Justine, you need a partner. One who cares about you. I have started to care about you. Let's do this together." He reaches for me and tries to pull me to him.

I'm shaking and can't find words. I stand up and go to the seat in the back of the plane and sit down. I speak loudly, even though I know he can hear me even if I don't.

"Leave me the fuck alone."

I turn the lights on. I go to the bathroom and wash my face and rub my breast where he has stroked me. I pull up my shirt and lift my bra and wash my breast. I start to cry. What the hell am I doing on this plane over the Atlantic Ocean with one of my own team members who is a predator?

I walk to the cockpit and notice that Thomas is now sitting in a seat toward the front of the plane with the seatback down and his eyes closed. Like this never happened?

"Hey Rich. Skip the London stop, okay? I want to land in Geneva and have Thomas get off there and then we will go on to Riyadh."

I want him to be put out without easy access to where he wants to go. I want him to know I'm in fucking charge.

"But I thought Colonel Coleman wanted to be in London."

"He can be in London. He can take a flight from Geneva." I smile without any joy and he nods. He looks at me, and I think he knows. Or maybe I just wish he knew.

I go back to my seat in the back corner of the plane and shut my eyes, but not before I put a suitcase on the seat next to me. My mind is reeling. What's the big deal? Why am I so upset? People are allowed to come on to people. And, when I said no, he didn't say anything or push me in any way. Grow up, Justine. Jesus.

But I know he assaulted me. I know it deep inside in a way that all of this has shown me. But not only that, he groomed me. Lured me into thinking he was on my team, which he is in some ways. I hate the confusion around it and so I only think about what actually happened, and how I have control over making sure it never happens again.

I sleep a bit and when I wake up two hours later, we are still a few hours outside of Geneva. He seems to still be asleep. I can't see his face but his seat is in the same position it had been in when I walked to the back of the plane.

It hits me. What I've read over the years about a person in a position of power, grooming someone who is vulnerable to them, and how easy it is to take advantage of them. I realize he had planned this all along. I wasn't sure when he started the plan, but I know he picked his time perfectly.

I had told him how grateful I was for what he'd shown me during the first part of the flight. He told me more than once over the past weeks that all I lacked was experience and he had that so all would be fine.

Rich announces on the intercom, "We will be landing in Geneva in an hour."

Henry comes back and puts out bagels, coffee and juice.

Thomas walks to the back of the plane to go to the bathroom. "Geneva?"

"Yes, Geneva," I say. "We are done."

I remind myself to think this through. Remind myself that I think he's critical to the success of what we're doing. That he's exceedingly good at what he does. That he is the reason they even found Caroline. I realize that I need to set a boundary, not create a holocaust.

I turn on my phone and text Robert.

> *Thomas came on to me. I will not be*
> *alone with him again. I understand*
> *how key he is to what we are doing.*
> *I do not need you to do anything.*

I know that keeping silent because of someone's stature, or because they have gifts to share that help you, is not an option. I know without proof that Thomas Coleman has used his brilliance, power and this "let me keep you safe" routine before.

I think about women in uniform and the stories that have come up repeatedly about how they are sexually abused, without agency to do anything about it. I know that it wouldn't have been as easy for the women he commanded to do what I did. Well, I did it. I'm not tired anymore, and I'm not scared.

We don't speak again and he gets off the plane without me even looking up. I see that he looks up at me in the window from the tarmac. I don't look away.

CHAPTER TWENTY-SEVEN

Sacrifice or Revenge

I arrive at the Four Seasons Hotel Riyadh mid-morning and check in. I know that there is likely a bug in the room, but I don't search for it. I assume I'm not alone and that I can capitalize on them thinking I don't know they're listening.

I text Tariq and he tells me they'll pick me up at 4 p.m. and I should dress for an outdoor café with burka. Caroline wants to meet in a public place and I think it's a good sign.

I'm tired and set my phone alarm for three hours. I figure I can order room service and be ready to go when the car comes for me.

I will myself to leave the Coleman incident behind and feel good about the fact that I'm not angry. Actually, I'm not anything and it feels new and freeing.

I think of Clarice, and how she didn't get mad when she was shut out of anything, or when someone was acting inappropriately. She just set her boundaries and kept the goal in mind. Restrained? Is that the word? Becoming Clarice is easier when the big picture could be life and death, and not sweating the small stuff takes on a new meaning.

I drift off and the next thing I know the alarm is going off. I order eggs and toast and take a shower and get dressed.

I can't see Caroline betraying me in an open café, but then again, maybe I'm not going to an open café at all. Or maybe she won't be there. That's my fear. That all might be lost and she'll disappear forever. I imagine Robert, and how that has to be what's keeping him up at night. One wrong move.

The drive from the hotel to the café is less than ten minutes. I could have walked. And I know exactly where it is. There is a doorway to a back terrace where there are a few tables with a lot of space between them. There is a fountain and it's loud. Between that and the burka barrier, the odds of being overheard are greatly reduced. I take out my "lipstick" device that tracks bugs and lay it on the table. It detects nothing.

She's late. It's been a half hour and she's still not here. I pull out my phone and look busy. I'm watching every inch of the café and relieved that I kept the garden wall behind me when I chose my chair. There are two women at a table on the other side of the garden and no one else. I see that the room inside is starting to fill up.

Caroline walks in the doorway in a way I can only describe as direct. Doesn't look to the left or to the right. Straight toward the table, and she takes the chair to my right that also has a wall behind it, so we are sitting kitty corner to each other.

She speaks to the waitress and then turns to me and says, "I've ordered tea and finger sandwiches and sweet treats for us, which will come at intervals. Do not speak when they are laying the food down but eat something so it doesn't appear that you are concerned about them."

She sits back and says nothing but seems to be surveying the area.

I lean forward. "Thank you for setting this up. I've been back to the U.S. and have seen your father, who I will tell you seems so much lighter than before I told him I spoke with you." I speak slowly and quietly.

She says nothing for a moment and then speaks calmly and succinctly. "I do not want to be rescued. I will never return to the States. I have a daughter who is attending Princeton. My husband will go for our daughter's graduation, but I will remain here. I will never leave Riyadh, and that is fine with me. What I care about is my children's future. That is *all* I care about. And they have a bright future surrounded by the love of their father and me. I will not sacrifice that for anything. You must make sure that is understood. I will never see my family in America again.

"But there *is* something I want. I know who my father has become. I know how powerful he is. I wondered if he would find me one day, and while I'm not surprised you came, I want to understand how you got here. I want to make sure no one else can find me. Tell me, and then I will tell you what I need."

She looks down when she is talking and I do the same. The sound of the waterfall next to us provides protection. She is calculating and she is cold. Not cold in an evil way, but distant and not connected. I realize she didn't ask about anyone in her family, or how her father is in general.

No one has dictated what I can and cannot say and I decide to tell her the truth. I also decide not to comment on her statement that she will never leave.

"There are retired government CIA, FBI and military people, men mostly, on the team who have put this together. But it is run by your father and the government has nothing to do with it. We have agents inside and they give us access to what we need.

"The woman who orchestrated your abduction, Ava, is in FBI custody from a sting operation that came out of her network being discovered by the agency who spends a lot more time watching the Saudis than they did before 9/11. Your father and his team saw this as an opportunity to get inside with me posing as Ava. I've met her, under the guise of being a psychiatrist brought in to evaluate her. I met with her at a hospital monitored and swept by our people. I have met with her twice. She has no idea that you are our focus."

I stop there. And I wait. Servers with food, tea and water arrive. I watch her without looking at her. Her body language is impossible to read and her face is covered. But she looks up at me and I meet her eyes. They are open but not saying anything. We both take a few bites.

"I'm assuming you know I am a wife to Sheik Habil. I assume you know how large a leap that is in my circumstances. I mentioned my daughter but what you might not know is that we also have a son. He's nine. He will inherit all that is his father's. There is no older son above him. I am lucky and entitled to help him take his place and be what he is being trained to be.

"My daughter, Amara, will graduate from Princeton and find her way to her own future, alongside her brother if they want that, but never married off to someone against her will. My children are everything to me, and I'm not interested in them knowing the origin of their parents' connection. Ever. If my father does anything to jeopardize their place in this life, I will never forgive him.

"I *am* interested, however, in them being monitored should something happen to me, to make sure they get what is theirs. I am confident that they are no threat to anyone and that Habil will set them up. He loves them, maybe more than me. They came later in life to him. I am his wife because I became pregnant, but also because I support him in a way he had no idea a woman could provide. That's all you need to know. That's all my father needs to know. Anything else that happened to me, or revenge, or retribution cannot happen. If it does, I will never forgive my father. Carry that message to him and then we will speak about what I want."

I say nothing. I think it's okay that I think for a moment and she continues to eat. So do I.

"I will fly back to America tomorrow and deliver your message to your father only, and come back right away. I want to know what your people think we are speaking about? Is it raising concern that you are meeting me?"

"My daily movements are not monitored. I am friends with many women who are here in my position. I have more freedom than I ever thought possible in the early years. The men don't want to know what's going on around the women coming in to serve them. They just want them to serve them the way they wish to be served.

"For some, it's not a problem. Women are amazing at adapting, I've learned. We've been doing it for centuries. Our bodies have always been our currency. For some, though, it's a problem."

I don't say anything.

She surprises me then by asking if I play backgammon. I say I do, and she asks our server to bring out a board. We set it up, and we play a few games. She plays well, but slowly. Almost like she doesn't want to appear to be too quick. I'm not sure.

We leave together and get in separate cars. I head back to the hotel, text Rich and tell him to meet me first thing in the morning at the airport.

I lie down to get some rest but can't find the peace I need. I'm not sure what time I fall asleep, but the next thing I know my alarm is going off and it's time to get ready to leave.

I'm anxious to speak with Robert. I have no idea what he'll say, but I know that I think she's right. I understand what she wants from him. She wants him to sacrifice what he wants. Revenge, her back in his world. I realize I have no idea how he will respond.

CHAPTER TWENTY-EIGHT

Thoughtfully Not Always Thoroughly

It always happens on the plane. I sit, and my mind takes a journey.

Today I'm thinking about some of the women who I socialize with, or used to when I was married. I know they are not attracted to their husbands. I know they are bought and paid for. I know that it's okay with them, which, of course, is nothing like what happened to Caroline, but the end result is similar. Quid pro quo.

I don't write a report to send to the team. I text Robert and tell him I will come over tonight when I land. Should be there by late afternoon. I want to shower first. And I want to do it at my home, not on the plane.

I remember every word Caroline said, but more important to me, I remember the way she said it. Either she's thought about this moment for a long, long time, or she practiced what she was going to say before we met for the second time. Or she is just certain about how she feels and doesn't care how anyone else feels.

I still marvel that she hasn't asked about her mother or asked me to send her father a message of caring. I have no idea what all that means, but I'm a bit in awe. Or sad, or I don't know what.

Rich walks down the aisle toward me. He is handsome, I think, and wonder if he was handsome before he was the one man I truly trusted here. He sits across from me.

"Am I disturbing you?" he asks.

"No, never. Not you, others maybe, but not you."

"I know you have a lot on your mind, and that things are moving quickly. I want you to know that keeping your own counsel is always a good thing. Thinking through the information and providing it to those around you should be done thoughtfully, not always thoroughly." He looks at me speculatively.

He can tell he's thrown me off guard.

"Wow. Didn't see that coming. What makes you say that, Rich?"

"I say that because I've been to this play more times than I can count, and I learned the hard lesson to evaluate those I'm speaking to before I decide what I'll share with them. It's one way to make sure you stay in control of what should be in your control."

"Has someone spoken to you about how I'm reporting information?" I ask.

"Well, if someone had spoken to me, I wouldn't tell you. But I will say this. You do have a few people around you who think you're making good decisions and think your influence on Robert could save lives, including yours. And that could mean mine." He smiles at me sort of tongue-in-cheek, and I am so filled with gladness at his presence right now that I almost tear up. But I know that less is more and so I respond, "Thanks."

He leans back but doesn't leave.

"Do you have a family, Rich?"

"No, I wouldn't do that to people. I can't live two lives without intertwining them and I know that with what I do, there's no sharing, so I don't. But I'm good."

And I know he is.

"Thank you for your candor. It will be with me as I move forward. You're right. I was thinking about what all this means in the bigger sense. Caroline doesn't want to come home. She is home and she likes what the future holds for her children, and there's no way she's tampering with that."

"Do you think she's thought about it all this time?"

"I don't know, but it's a great question. I think she thinks about everything. And she does it fast. And I can see she weighs things carefully, more carefully than I do, and I can see how well that serves her."

We sit quietly reflecting separately.

"You know in backgammon there's a lot of luck," I say. "Skill too but there's also luck. You weigh the odds, and you do it quickly and then you make the best move you can, recognizing that the outcome of your move might have nothing to do with the brilliance of your play and everything to do with the dice over which you have no control.

"Caroline and I played backgammon this last visit and I can see that she plays a lot. And I can see she likes it, and I can tell by the way she moves the checkers she understands the game. When I returned to my hotel afterwards, I thought maybe she approaches her life and backgammon the same way. She makes the best calculated move she can and accepts the outcome, which might be outside the parameters of what her move could provide."

We eat dinner together and don't speak of much. When we land, I put my hand on his shoulder when I leave the plane and say, "Thanks, Rich." He knows it's not a thank you for the flight.

CHAPTER TWENTY-NINE

How Calculating

Robert doesn't say anything. Nothing, after I tell him what she said. He asks if she said anything else about her son.

"I told you everything, Robert. She was clear. Succinct. No emotion. She reminds me a bit of you." I smile at him but he doesn't notice.

I continue, "We played backgammon. Did you teach her?"

"No, I did not."

Backgammon is bigger in the Middle East than it is in the States or Europe. I have a feeling she plays with the sheik. I would like to ask her if she beats him.

He gets up, leaves the library and comes back,

sits down, and says, "I want you to go and observe Amara at Princeton. See what she is like. I want to see just how happy she is."

If you can't save the mother, save the child of the mother? Seriously? Could he be that calculating? I think he could, actually, but he wouldn't call it that.

I tell him I will go the next day if he sets it up. I tell him I want to bring Julia from the team so it's not a single person wandering around stalking her. And because Julia was trafficked, she might notice something I don't. He agrees.

I wait a moment and then say, "Robert, where are you going with this? You know if you take Amara, Caroline will be killed. Right? You know that."

He just looks at me, gets up and leaves.

CHAPTER THIRTY

I Wish I Had What She Has

We drive ourselves from the Princeton Airport and make our way along the tree-lined road and over the bridge, where the river is filled with Princeton rowers practicing. I'd forgotten how beautiful the campus is. I know the campus. My high school boyfriend went there, and I visited him a number of times. That was over thirty years ago. Nothing has changed.

We know exactly where to go to see Amara in her daily routine. First, a class where Julia and I can sit and audit in the back, and then a study group she attends in the lobby of one of the dorms. No following her. We will have two opportunities to observe her, and that's it.

I know someone must be following her now, and I wonder whether they will be here today and if Robert has standing orders to pick her up if he gives the call. Abduction. First the daughter? Then the granddaughter?

We are in class before she comes in. She walks in with two other students and they are laughing and talking and take seats together toward the front.

She is stunning. Tall, like her mom, fine features but dark, which I imagine mirrors her father. It's a striking combination and I see in her the same confidence that her mother had in the picture Robert showed me when he first spoke of Caroline.

She participates in the class. Smart participation. It's a literature class and they're studying effective altruism. I'm in awe of the dialog going on after a reading they all did around the difference between ineffective altruism and effective altruism. I smile to myself as I realize this was worth the trip alone.

Amara makes the point that sometimes you won't know when you begin the altruistic journey whether the outcome is worth it or not. And her feeling is you shouldn't spend too much time evaluating it before, but rather during, and then change direction should you need to based on the outcome you desire.

Lesson learned by me, Amara. I have no idea if what I'm doing is altruistic or self-serving to a man who wants his daughter back.

Most of the group heads out after the class, and we hang back before going over to sit in the dorm lounge area, which is filled with students. Strangely, we aren't out of place at all. Then she walks in with a coffee and sits with her peers. She's engaged in conversations we can't hear, but they are there for two hours going over notes, laughing, and even arguing, or so it seems.

We leave, and I know I'll tell Robert that this young woman is not, in my limited opinion based on little information, in trouble emotionally. I'm sure of it. Or as sure as a stranger can be.

Robert calls me on the plane as soon as we take off from Princeton's airport.

"Well?"

"Well, my friend, she is quite something." I tell him about her in the class and how she mirrors the strong young women she is engaging with.

"Leave her alone, Robert. Her mother seems to have given her what she needs to be a modern woman in a man's world that is her legacy now. Leave her alone."

He tells me he will see me later, and we hang up. I turn to Julia.

"What do you think?"

"I think I wish I'd had what she has," she says.

She gets on her phone and I'm on mine the rest of the trip.

That night, I sit thinking about what Amara might know. Has her mother told her anything? I don't think she has. Does it matter? Let go of what you can't know, or don't need to know, Justine. Namaste.

CHAPTER THIRTY-ONE

I Never Knew Her

The meeting with the team the next day is brief. I'm to tell Caroline that her father will honor her request. Robert isn't there and I'm told that he will meet with me afterward.

I've already decided I'm going in and telling Caroline we will do what she wants. Whatever it is.

Robert and I have lunch after the meeting and it's obvious he doesn't want to discuss the decision. As we finish up, I decide I want to tell him I respect what he's doing.

"I think it takes a lot for a man like you to let go of something you have spent a few decades searching to recapture. I think you are making the right decision."

"Let's play backgammon," is his only response.

So, we play backgammon. All afternoon. He's aggressive and taking risks. I'm not. I make plays without giving into impulse and I realize that I've learned a lot about doing the right thing, sticking to the plan, or in the case of backgammon, the moves with the best odds of winning.

And I like this new me. Calculated. Smart. Sure-footed and willing to accept the consequences of my moves; realizing that the outcome is out of my hands and with the luck gods that oversee all play. But also not in a hurry.

I can envision a life moving forward, living at a slower pace. More thoughtful about many things, especially how I spend my time and with whom.

Before I get up to leave, Robert looks at me, leans back and takes a deep breath. I lean forward aware that he has something to say.

"I'm sure you must have wondered how I came to my decision. I had no interest in discussing it with you but I think you deserve to know why I've decided to do what Caroline wants.

"All these years, all these miserable years, I have conjured up in my mind a hell that she was living, which in some ways was worse than thinking she didn't make it.

"I felt responsible, not for what happened, or that she got picked up, but that with all my brains and power and wealth and connections, I couldn't find her. It was inconceivable to me that she could be alive and not be found. It haunted me. Everywhere I went, I wondered if she was nearby. Everyone I met, I wondered if they knew something I didn't.

"I didn't know her. I didn't pay any attention to her. She was entertainment when I had the time. She was there during holidays but I had no real interest in her. Not until she was gone and then I realized that enjoying watching her when she was in my presence wasn't entertainment; it was love. And I also knew that I had no idea who she was or who she could become or what she thought about, well, about anything.

"And then we find her. But then you come with this demand from her that I leave her and her children alone. And I realize that I *like* her decisions. And I'm so goddamn proud of who she is, and how she got out of her hell without any help from anyone, that I cannot contain myself.

"And I feel like I know her now, more than I did when she lived in the same house as me. I know she is cunning and smart and a survivor, and that she cares more about her kids than I did, and that I will do whatever she asks.

"Maybe I'm telling you this now, not because you deserve to know, and you do, but because I want someone to look at me, and tell me that I'm right. That this person is extraordinary. Beautiful. Someone anyone would be proud to call their daughter. I am proud and I want someone to know it."

I look at him for a long moment. He isn't emotional, as much as he seems curious, wanting me to answer him. So I do.

"I am in awe of her, and when I see what you are doing for her now, I know you are cut from the same cloth. You have every reason to be proud."

He pushes back from the table and says, "See you tomorrow, Justine."

I sit there awhile looking at the setting sun and I wonder how I could be so lucky as to be in this place, at this moment, doing this for a few special, wondrous people. It must be fifteen minutes before I get up and go home. Maybe longer.

CHAPTER THIRTY-TWO

Three Turns from Where They Took Me

In the middle of the flight back to tell Caroline
about Robert's decision, a text comes in from Tariq.
> *My people will meet your flight to take*
> *you to a meeting.*
The team wants to turn the plane around.
I say no. Robert takes ten minutes to decide.
Ten minutes. It's not lost on me that he will take
chances with my life if it means possibly saving
Caroline, and I'm good with that.

Hours later, Rich touches the plane down, but
it feels like minutes. I'm struck with how gentle he
always is with this majestic bird. I can feel the way
he kindly brings the wheels and the fuselage back
to earth, as if they were fragile, and I think on some

233

level he does it that way for me. I know that my fear of flying disappears when he's in charge.

Rich pulls over to our spot on the tarmac, and there are two SUVs waiting. I sit up straight. *Pay attention, Justine.* Henry opens the door and unfolds the steps. Six men get out of the two cars and head over to the plane. I've never seen any of them. They are dressed in robes. Rich looks at me, and I smile and wave him off. "I'm good."

I walk down the steps with Henry following and I note that Rich is right behind him, when normally he stays on the plane. I know he's armed. Not a lot of good that will do. One of the men steps forward. He's fat. It's all in his front, and when he walks he leads with his stomach. His lips are wet. I hate men with wet lips. They remind me of my stepfather, who, when he kissed me hello, left a wet spot on my cheek that I always rushed to rub off with my sleeve.

He shakes my hand, and I notice that his nails are not smooth. They are sort of ragged, and I know that something is not right. It's that sixth sense they told me about. Danger.

"I am Adil and I am here to take you to meeting with investors."

I say nothing but hold out my hand to indicate

he should lead the way. I'm put in the back of the second car, alone, and there is a partition I can't see through between the driver's seat and the back seat.

I turn back to Rich before they close the door and decide to give him the signal.

"Rich, I shouldn't be more than four or five hours. Please have some lunch and get the plane ready to go. I'll call you if anything changes."

That's the signal for, "If you don't hear from me in five hours, do what you can. Something's wrong."

I flash back to one of our flights in the dead of night early on, when Rich and I went over signals. I remember saying to him, "If I say that and you don't hear from me, what you should do is get the hell out of Dodge." We both laughed at his response. "I live in Dodge. I love Dodge. No way I'm getting out of Dodge without you."

I knew this might happen. Did Caroline sound the alarm? Are they now questioning why I'm showing up after all these years? Or are they actually having a meeting? Or something else I haven't thought of?

We pull up to an unfamiliar compound surrounded by a tall stucco wall. Before the driver puts the car in park, the gate opens and two more men come outside, looking back and forth as if there could possibly be someone following.

I can feel my face getting red. When I get nervous, I don't sweat, but my face gets red. I put on my burka. High on my nose so my eyes are barely showing. I get out of the car and follow both men in. The cars seem to be staying. I think that's a good sign, but maybe I'm just looking for a good sign. I'm not shaking but I can hardly breathe. Breathe in. Breathe out. Slowly. Keep your heart rate down.

We walk down a long corridor and into a room. It looks like a gynecologist's office, including the stirrups at the end of an examination table. Only this table doesn't have the paper on it that rolls down for patient after patient. And it's not clean. There is a man standing inside waiting for us.

"Ms. Lloyd, take off all your clothes and lie down on the table."

"Are you going to leave the room?" I ask trying to keep my voice calm. "Is there a sheet I can put over me?"

"No."

I put my bag on the chair and that's when I see it. It's in the corner of the ceiling, and it's a camera. I'm sure of it, and I'm also sure that someone is watching. I'm fucking sure of it, and I am filled with such loathing for the evil creatures these men are I'm no longer frightened.

Fuck them. Fuck them all. It's about power. I know it's about power, and I know they know that I know they are watching. This all comes to me in a split second. I turn and look into the camera with a "go ahead" look on my face.

My body was never great. And now it's overweight, and I'm not a proud woman with perky breasts or legs that are toned the way they were in days gone by. Then I look at the man standing there waiting, and I notice that he's biting his lip and that his fat is much worse than mine, and I hate him even more. I take off my clothes quickly and lie on the table, face up.

I look at the ceiling, not at the camera. Actually, I've been prepped for this. "Take yourself somewhere else. Count something." I see that the ceiling has those tiles with dotted indentions in them. I count across the top row. Then I count down the rows on that tile. Then I count how many tiles go across the ceiling. Then I count the width of the ceiling and how many tiles are there. I try and do the multiplication in my head. It's hard to do, while my body is being invaded in a way I never contemplated. But it is quicker than I think, and I'm grateful for the diversion, and even though I have no idea how many small holes are in that celling, I know that each and every one of them took in a piece of my trauma.

Months later, I wonder at how many other women's traumas sit in those small holes as well. And I surmise that I was probably luckier than most with my outcome. I honor them with a mantra. *We are not without power, not now, no matter what they do to us.*

He does what they told me might be done if I was searched. And then some. He touches my entire body. He rubs my nipples, and they retreat in horror and when I think about it, I'm so proud of them.

I realize how much a woman's body responds to the man himself. This thought has given me solace when the nightmares started after the entire thing was over. I remind myself when I wake up terrified over and over again, that my breasts were the strongest part of me that awful morning; the only part that could show real resistance.

He touches everywhere but I'm not afraid. I just want it to be over. Then he scratches me with his ragged nails. On the side of my left breast. The mark did not leave a scar, and I was grateful for that, too. It would have been more than I could bear.

He takes his time. When he tells me to spread my legs, I say, "I'm happy to do that but you will not put your unwashed hands inside me without gloves." I say it for the men watching. Fuck them.

He pauses and I can feel his anger, his rage. I have humiliated him. I'm angry now too. He walks over to the cabinet, takes out gloves and puts them on. Then he comes back and I shut my mind down and he does what he needs to do.

In retrospect, I don't think he got any pleasure out of it, and I also know that it's all about the cowards on the other side of the lens above me. It's about men who get off on buying slaves and women who have no choice.

"Roll over and get on your hands and knees."

I have reached my limit. I snap.

"No!" And I sit up and try to get off the table. That's when he grabs me and shoves me down. He grabs me by the arms, and it's a searing pain as I feel the blood vessels inside my arms cringe. He is so much stronger than me and his rage at my lack of submission has made him even stronger. The black and blue marks of that moment were there for two months. That's a long time.

I know this is about power, and I know he is angry and I don't care in that moment. I never believe through any of it that he will hurt me. Not physically anyway. I believe on some level I'm physically safe because I'm the provider of women for men much higher up than him.

I decide I've had enough. "We are done here. Either you take me to the meeting, if there is one, or back to the plane. But we are done here."

I'm surprised at my voice. It's deeper than normal. It's not quick the way it usually is when I'm making a point. It's not mine. It's firm.

He looks at me.

The phone rings, he picks it up, says nothing, hangs up, turns to me and says, "You can put your clothes back on."

And he walks out the door.

I never saw him again. But in the dead of night when it's pitch black in my room and I've just awakened from one of my recurring nightmares, I see him clearly. On those nights he's scarier than he was that day. Much more frightening because he knows I know he's weak. And, because he lost the battle for power that day, I fear he will seek revenge, not with me who is out of reach, but with his wife, a slave, a daughter, or the next woman who ends up in that room without the power I had. That's what haunts me. That my behavior will be the price another woman pays.

He's gone, but I know I'm not alone. I know they're still watching. I want to show I'm in control so I don't hurry. I get up slowly and put my clothes on and brush my hair. A woman walks in, wearing a burka, and I follow her out, into an elevator, and then down another set of hallways into a chamber-like waiting room.

A door opens, and I walk in. Tariq is there, but he's not in charge. Another man is and he doesn't introduce himself. He is dressed in a dark, well-cut Western suit.

I look him in the eye. He is not kind. I know it instantly. He's cold, sociopathic, with a cruel edge. I decide to speak first. "I know who you are. You're the broker. I supply the girls and you control their fate, the final word as to where they end up. Powerful.

"And you and I both know you were watching me just now. Most likely enjoying my humiliation. But let me remind you, you do not control me. We are business partners, equals. If you ever do that to me again, we are done. Me, and the money and the women. We will all be gone."

He sits across from me, showing no reaction.

"We have worked with you for decades," he says. "You have changed all the rules and the way you are doing everything. You tell us you are expanding and moving here and to Dubai. You want to work with women already here. This might work for all of us, but we need to be sure you are not representing someone else who doesn't have the same interests we have had all these years."

My turn to not react.

I look out the window and say, "This is the most amazing garden I've ever seen." And it is. Stunning. Simple. Green. Lush.

I pause. He says nothing. No one is looking directly at me, but everyone is paying attention.

I go on. I have no idea where it comes from. "I'm the one who should be searching you. I have felt all these years that our arrangement was with a few individuals. That even where the women ended up did not lead back to me. I felt sheltered, known only to a few trusted individuals, like Tariq.

"Then my country elects a new president who you think you can call friend, and I'm compromised. You can't trust him. You think you can, but he's a loose cannon, which in American English means you will never know where the cannonball is set to land and destroy until it's fired. And, if it's been turned on you, you won't have time to get out of the way. I'm moving my operation because I don't intend to be caught in the crossfire."

No one says anything. Nor do I. For a few minutes. A cell phone rings in the pocket of the man in charge, he gets up, leaves the room and we all wait for his return.

He returns and says, "I think we are done here. I do have one more question before we take you to your hotel. When are the two women going to be delivered?"

I answer, "As soon as I can safely get them out of the United States. They are ready. It's my new safety measures that are taking some extra time. I want to close down my operation in the U.S. and move it to Dubai, as you know. I am as anxious as you are to get them settled here so I can finish what I need to there."

He nods and walks out of the room with everyone except one man, who has sat in the back of the room for the entire time. He walks over to me, says nothing and ushers me out of the room, down two hallways and out to a courtyard. He opens the back passenger door of a car that is parked there, waves me in, then gets

into the driver's seat and immediately heads out
to the street.

"Are we going to my hotel?"

"Yes," the driver answers.

I turn on my phone and text Rich.

> *Heading to the hotel. Mark where I*
> *am now please. I am three turns from*
> *where they took me. A left, and about*
> *a mile later, a right and then two*
> *blocks later, a left. I'm fine. Will text*
> *from the hotel as soon as I get there.*

CHAPTER THIRTY-THREE

Someone on the Other End

I have a few hours before I have to meet
Caroline. I shower. A long shower. I scrub my body
until it's raw and red and hurts, but I don't feel
clean. I'm not sure how that will work over time,
but I'm going to make sure I don't dwell there.

I lie down, order room service, eat ice
cream and a salad; the ice cream first just
because, and I rest.

I feel good when I walk outside to go to the
cafe to meet Caroline. I don't need them to drive
me. It's a ten-minute walk from the hotel and I
want to walk. I stroll along amidst all the people
hurrying somewhere and wonder at how everyone
has a destination that means something different.

"What did he say?" she asks the moment I sit down across from her. She has been waiting and this is the most anxious I've seen her.

"Your father said he will do whatever you want. And, Caroline, I have known him a long time. I'm surprised he isn't asking what you want him to do before agreeing to it. I think he wants you to know that he is on your side, whatever you need."

She sits back in her chair. I can feel the weight coming off her. Then she pauses and says to me, "Do you believe him?"

"Yes, I do. I totally do. And it's costing him personally."

She takes a few minutes to pull herself together. Food arrives. We start to eat in silence. Then she speaks. Softly, her weariness apparent.

"There is a good friend, Kamaria, who was taken around the same time I was. She is in a desperate situation. I want you to extract her. Get her out. I want you to eliminate the sheik who has her. He is cruel and vicious and offers nothing to anyone. He has been a kingpin in this region for over two decades and has been instrumental in many, many abductions and unspeakable, sadistic acts."

She gives me his name, Sheik Faliz. Her voice carries a growing strength and I can feel her anger.

"Several of his women have disappeared without a trace over the years with a few of them found dead, severely beaten, on the streets. He claims they ran away and he can't be responsible for what happens to them after they leave his 'protection.' I believe my friend Sophie might have been one of these women. It would have been early on when I was in no position to try to help her."

I feel her guilt, devastation and subsequent resolve. My heart hurts.

She tells me that the two new women I'm supposed to be bringing in have been purchased by him. She thinks delivery of them might be a good way to go in. "It will get you in the door, and then you can get to Kamaria to get her out."

She is so clear and smart and thorough. Like her dad.

"What are you telling your people we're going to do together?"

"I'm telling them you have told me how to work with the women having problems and that I can come back to you if I need to, but I don't quite trust you to meet with the women yourself. I think it's better if I do it myself.

"I need to remove myself from what you're going to do, so I'm not suspected of anything," she continues. "I'm confident I will be fine. People see what they want to see, and Habil wants me to be who I have been all these years. He trusts me and will not look at any other alternative."

"Who will be my contact to make sure Kamaria knows we are coming and when?"

"You can text me at this number," and she reads out a number that I memorize. "I will take care of making sure everything is in place at the compound."

"Caroline, I have to ask. Not for your father, but for me. Are you okay? How do you do this?"

She looks at me without saying anything for quite a while. I take another bite of my tea sandwich and a sip of the iced tea and wait.

"I'm not sure what you mean. I was so young. I don't even know for sure what those early years were like. But now I have a life that I can live, with a man who has always been kind to me. I imagine he doesn't think about how he got to me. I think about it all the time.

"But I have two amazing children, who I love so deeply and am so proud of. My daughter is so much more aware than I ever was. She cares about so many wonderful things; literature, women's rights in this country that she knows is behind the times. She has her father wrapped around her smile and she will always have freedom. He and I have spoken, and if she needs to live in England to have a full life, that will happen. She already has enough money there to do what she wants, so if something happens to him or me, she can never be put in a closet marriage. It was a deal that I secured long ago and we both know how great her life can be.

"And, my son, who is being groomed to take over for his father, is being trained to be a good man. He will never buy anyone, and I do not believe he knows his father ever did. I was the last person he got that way, and I can move beyond it. Not forgive it, but know that I want to spend my energy on that which I can control; and so all of my efforts have gone toward my children."

"Do you follow your father? Do you know what he does?"

"I do sometimes. Not often. That was a long time ago, and I wasn't close to him. I got what I wanted from him, silly things that don't matter, but I can't remember a real conversation he and I ever had. I do not totally trust him because I know his power and his methods. I saw them with my

mother. I never wanted the marriage they had."
She stops, turns her head slightly and gives me a
trace of a smile. "Or the one I have."

We both take a moment, then she
continues, "You seem to know my father. Do
you think I can trust that he will leave Amara alone?
That he will not expose me, ever? What about if I
died? Would he do something then?"

I need to think about that. I want to be honest.

"I don't know. I know he will watch all of
you. I know that. But he has exceptional people
working for him and they will never expose you.

"I do think he understands why you are doing
what you are doing. It's quite selfless. But I will give
him my phone, the one I have now and you have
the number. He will have it with him and he will be
a phone call away. I think that might be enough.
But I can't promise what he will do. But if I had to
say, I would say if he was going to do it, he would
do it now and he is not going to do it now. He will
do what you ask."

She smiles at me. Neither one of us is ready
to say good-bye. She speaks first. "Should we play
some backgammon?" We play. For more than an
hour. We smile across the table. We don't speak of
anything but I am so grateful to have this time with

her. To see that I think she is where she wants to be; that she has come to terms with who she has become and feels good about it. On some level she is living the life that was taken from her in the best way she can. She is lovely.

It's time to go, but before I get up from the table, I feel the need to say one more thing. "I think you are an amazing woman. Remember that the number you have will always have someone on the other end who cares about what happens to you and to your children. It's been a gift to have some time with you."

She has her burka on again. I can't see her smile, but I can see her eyes are wet and I look away. We are done. I get up and walk out the door without looking back.

I text Tariq and tell him I'm headed back to the States and will deliver the two women in a week or so and can meet with the women they are concerned about after I deliver the two new ones; but that the woman he had me meet, Sakirah, can probably do it herself if they want, and I can work with her. I tell him I gave her some pointers based on what she described and I think it's not a problem long term.

I'm on the plane an hour later. I sleep the entire way home.

CHAPTER THIRTY-FOUR

You Need to Know Three Things

The team has had three days to plan everything. Three days. My mind races, thinking about Caroline, who is waiting to hear the final details from me, wondering whether her father will truly do what she is asking. Weighing the risks to her and her children.

I think she must be sure of her position there to be willing to set this up with us. Or she might assess our plan and determine there is too much risk to her after all. Or maybe she can't bear the thought of the women in the control of this monster and isn't measuring the risk clearly.

I realize I want to do this for her. I want to get Kamaria out. I want this despicable abuser to get the justice he deserves. I take a deep breath and pull into the driveway, ready to hear what they've put together.

Part of me wants it to be over and done; in the plane waiting for everyone to load up and fly away. But there's another part of me that wants to be part of this. I want to continue to explore the Clarice I've found inside of me.

I want to stare into the eyes of those men as we bring them down. I want to put my arms around Kamaria when we're getting her out and tell her that she's brave and it's over and she will get better.

But maybe that's just part of the fantasy of who I think I've become rather than who I am. Most likely what I want to do, or think I can do, will not be on the table. I know I've made progress with the White Socks Posse, my new name for the men on the team, but I also know they surely don't think of me as an agent, or as having the tools to have a real role in this.

I pull up and Thomas Coleman is waiting in the driveway. Standing there, waiting. I sit in the car for more seconds than is comfortable before I turn the engine off, get out and walk over to him. I stand in front of him and wait for him to speak.

"Before we are all together, I want you to know that I am deeply sorry for how I behaved and what happened on the plane that night. I think I was carried away in the moment, but it doesn't represent the man I am. Robert said I am here because you agreed that it was the right thing for the mission. It *is* the right thing, and I am confident in the plan and everything surrounding it. I hope we can work together through these next few days."

I remind myself I do not have to make him comfortable. I have to be comfortable.

"First of all, your apology, with the addition that your behavior is not who you are, doesn't move me in the least. It's exactly who you are, and I have a feeling it's worked well for you in your career filled with women who didn't have the power I did on that airplane. Every time I think of it, I'm proud that I did what they did not have the agency to do.

"Here's what you need to know. Three things. One: I've told no one other than Robert what happened, but that's not a guarantee I won't tell anyone else in the future. Two: I will never be in a room alone with you again, and any woman on the team will not either. And the third thing is most important. If I ever hear a story about you in the press, or you ever deny the accusation of someone who outs you for who we both know you are, and you try to squash her like a bug, I will out you. I've already set it up.

"You and I were on Robert's plane going to Europe and … well, you know the 'and.' I want you to remember that. But I also think you are an amazing mind and incredible resource for this work. That is more important than either one of us right now, so I am grateful you are on the team.

"You have no power over me, and I now have all the power over you that a girl needs to keep herself and others safe."

I turn around without waiting for an answer of any kind and walk into the house. I go to the ladies room and look in the mirror. Good talk.

CHAPTER THIRTY-FIVE

She-KK *and* Home

I head to the meeting room where everyone, including Robert, is there. There's an empty seat next to Chip and an empty seat next to Coleman. I take the seat next to Coleman and survey the room. Everyone is weary, some are disheveled, but each and every person at the table is also wide awake and you can tell they're excited to get started.

Jason begins.

"We have a solid plan. It's a double operation. Two locations, same timing, one to take out Sheik Faliz and one to extract the woman from the compound in Riyadh.

"Turns out that Faliz is going to be on his

yacht this weekend. That's in six days. And we think taking him out on the yacht is the best way to accomplish both missions with the least amount of exposure. And, in case you're concerned that he doesn't deserve what he's getting, we have intel that says he backs terrorists. He's a bad character, and we are good with this ending for him.

"Routinely, he takes only a few of his security detail on the yacht with him. He feels secure there, and the surprise element is perfect. We anticipate that his yacht will be moored about an hour off the coast of Bahrain.

"We will have a rented yacht, the *Sirius*, anchored about two miles away. We will send in three Zodiacs with four team members each, and an additional Zodiac that will stand off-site in case it's needed."

I interrupt. "I don't know what a Zodiac is. Can you be sure to speak layman's English? Thank you."

Thomas steps in. "Some are used commercially, but in this case a Navy Zodiac is a specially fabricated rubber inflatable boat used by the military for an operation like this.

"We'll have all retired Navy SEALs on this part of the mission and they are going through the drills off the coast of South Carolina as we speak. They're leaving tonight to get into place."

"Sorry, Justine," Jason continues. "We will launch one team from the stern and one from the bow and the other will wait at midship until both the stern and the bow teams are in place. They will take out the security people on the decks and secure the bridge and then move midship to let the rest of the team on."

He passes out sheets of paper with the drawing of a rather large yacht and points to two figures sleeping in a bed located midship. There are other bedrooms, crew's quarters, mess hall, dining room and three living room areas.

"We're not sure how many people will be on the boat. We'll determine the final details based on how many board when they leave port. Our plan is to take out the sheik, drug and tie up his wife or mistress, whoever is with him, and then exit the yacht. All within ten minutes of the mission's start. If anyone wakes up, we will restrain and temporarily drug them.

"Once this is accomplished, the team will return to the *Sirius* which will move on to the port in Abu Dhabi. Some of the team will exit there and head to their designated destinations. The *Sirius* will continue on to Dubai, where the rest will disembark and make their way to Europe and the United States. The code name for the operation is *She-KK*."

He takes a breath but no one speaks. We are waiting for the second part. I sit there thinking that maybe it's a good thing the sheik will not be in the compound at the same time the woman is being rescued. Yes, it's definitely a good thing. Karma? Luck? Either way, I'll take it. *She-KK*. What does that stand for? Sheik Kill? No need to ask.

"The second part of the plan is more complicated. I will turn it over to Anthony to review."

More complicated? Seriously?

"Thanks, Jason. First of all, we are hoping to launch at the first location at zero one hundred hours. But that will depend on when the sheik's yacht shuts down for the night and everyone appears to be asleep.

"We are placing receptors in all the rooms on the yacht so we should know when everything is quiet, but either way, we hope it will be about 1 a.m. We want both of these operations to launch simultaneously, so the timing will be determined by the action on the yacht."

Thomas steps in again. "Rich will be at the airport running the Riyadh operation. He will be backed up by me in Dubai. We will both be on the same channel in case Rich has to step aside. The code name for Riyadh is *Home*."

I start to choke up. Just a little.

Anthony continues, "Justine, you are going to send an email to Tariq telling him you will be delivering the two new women to the sheik's compound on Saturday at around 1 in the morning. You will bring them in a van and they will be helped in by your team. The van will have two female agents posing as these women, helped in by two more agents.

"We are hopeful that Tariq will open the door without more than one person in attendance. The household shuts down early each night, especially when the sheik is not there. Justine, you must be there for this part of the mission. We don't think Tariq will let anyone else in without being alerted that something is off.

"Depending on how many of Tariq's men are present, we will disarm and restrain them. We will go to the designated bedroom, get Kamaria out and leave.

"One member of the team will wait in the van

driver's seat with another in the back of the van. Once Kamaria is extracted, she will be loaded in the back of the van along with Justine and the two female agents.

"Everyone will be transported to the airport where Rich will be ready for takeoff. It's not the King Khalid Airport, but the National Guard Airport right outside of town. We have people in place there and the king has allowed the airport to be used in the past for transporting sensitive cargo and other ops. No one will question the plane waiting or taking off without fanfare."

The room is quiet.

Robert says, "Lunch will be brought in now and Thomas, Justine and I are going to have lunch outside. We will regroup here in forty-five minutes. I have two questions I want answered when we return. What can go wrong and what will we do if it does? And what is the risk that Caroline will be implicated in this when they review it?"

CHAPTER THIRTY-SIX

She Needs to be There

We don't speak until they set our lunch plates down and leave the patio area. I click the tab on my Diet Coke, pouring it into the glass of ice, just the way I like it, and then turn my attention to the lobster salad. I idly think about how I like the claw of the lobster but not the tail, which is considered the best part. People like that about me because I'm willing to trade a tail for just one claw. Win-win. I look up at Robert and Thomas.

Robert speaks first. "Two assurances I want before we go back in there and I assume you have considered both. Is Justine safe to do this, and will Caroline be considered as a part of it by anyone?"

Thomas takes a moment to chew the bite of food in his mouth before responding. "Not having Justine there, her failure to show up, would raise a red flag that could compromise the entire operation.

"We considered all of it. She needs to be there so Tariq doesn't suspect a setup. If she isn't with them when they arrive, I don't think he will let them in. I wouldn't. While Ava wasn't in attendance in the past, she has now made it clear she's in the field. And if she says she isn't coming, he might be okay with that initially but he will be on guard and might add extra security.

"She has proven herself and they trust her. They trust the administration. They are not concerned, especially in their own neighborhood, that this is not just two more women being dropped off like all the times before.

"Justine needs to be there and I think it will go well; and our guys in the van will take off with her in the back of the van at the slightest sign of trouble. We will also have another van a block away to pull in to extract the others, but only if there's trouble. We don't want additional vehicles coming and going to raise suspicion. I think this is as safe as it can be, but Justine can say no right here, and we will change the plan."

He continues, "As far as Caroline, I do not think she will be implicated, nor does Jason. She is now truly trusted. She has traveled to London to shop and took the kids with her. She had security but not the kind that says they have any idea she would run. And, Robert, she didn't run.

"She hasn't reached out to anyone before. They are committed to her, as she is to them, and I believe she is safe. Her husband is powerful enough that no one will contemplate looking at her from the inside and he will not either. I think this plan is a strong one. We lucked out that Sheik Faliz is on his yacht this weekend. Everyone on the team, *everyone*, feels strongly that we have this covered. And that now is the time to go in."

Robert looks over at me. "Justine, do you want to do this?"

I look directly at each of them. "Yes," I answer, picking out a part of the claw from my salad for my next bite.

CHAPTER THIRTY-SEVEN

Quid Pro Quo

I head home and swim laps. I sit on my deck overlooking the pool and I'm uncomfortable, and I don't know why.

I call Robert.

"I want to go see Ava one more time before we do the operation. I need to try one more time to get more information from her. I will go tomorrow if you can make it work. I need this, Robert."

I get a text from Chip in an hour saying to be at the Palm Beach Airport at 8 a.m. the next morning.

Wheels are up. We will land in D.C. in an hour and a half. My mind is spinning. Tomorrow I leave for a black ops mission, to extract a woman I've never met, from a compound I've never been to, to save her from an abusive man who probably paid a million dollars for her years ago.

We're doing it at the behest of my friend's daughter, who has no desire to save herself, which was the entire point of all of this in the first place. And, instead of spending this last day working with the team to make sure I'm as safe as I can be, I decide to fly to Washington to speak one more time to Ava.

I'm not even sure why I feel the need to do this, or what I want from her, or how I will get it. Our last meeting wasn't all that productive, but there was a glimmer, and for some reason, I think this is my last opportunity to see her and find out what I don't know but seem to have a burning desire to know. Self-doubt creeps in.

What do I want? I think about it. I want to know why she did what she did. Why do I want to know it, I demand of myself. I surmise that in order to feel safe playing her perhaps I need to get in deeper. But I know that isn't it. I ponder the possibility that I want to know what happened to her because I want to think there is a reason that will be understandable to me in explaining, maybe even accepting, who she became and the horrors of what she did.

I understand the men. Their need for power over women because of whatever makes them feel so less than. I get it. Hate it. But get it. But I can't wrap my mind around her.

Ava has a history. I feel compelled to try one more time to find out what it is.

I lay my head back and recline the seat. I shut my eyes, clear my mind, and then I think of it. Clarice and Hannibal Lecter. She wanted him to help her. She chose to give him information about herself, even after her superior warned her, "Clarice, you don't want Hannibal Lecter in your head." Quid pro quo, Hannibal labeled it.

I wonder if there is something Ava might want that I can give. Ava would like the idea of quid pro quo. She'd like it because it would make allowing herself to be vulnerable palatable. Less personal.

Rich comes back to talk.

"What are we doing here?" he asks.

"I want to find out why Ava did what she did. I don't know why I need to know exactly, but I do. I know it sound nuts, especially considering what we are doing tomorrow."

He sits looking at me for a moment, smiles and says, "No it doesn't, actually. It's dotting every 'i' and crossing every 't,' which is what a good agent does before walking into an unknown danger arena. You're right to do it."

He stands up and walks back to the cockpit. I can tell he instinctively knows that I need to be by myself to think.

We land an hour later, and I arrive at the facility and am ushered into the same room as usual. But this time, I take out my sweeper and go through the room looking for a bug or a camera. I want to make sure it will be me and Ava without anyone else listening.

It's all clear.

Ava walks in, sits down, looks across the table at me and this time I can see she is curious. Maybe we both thought the last meeting was our final one.

I decide to get right to it. "Ava, I asked for this meeting because I don't want to leave here, or be finished with our interactions, until I know why you did what you did. I'm not sure why I want to know, but there it is. For some reason, I don't think you did it for the money, as you intimated in our last session. Maybe that makes me a Pollyanna, but I don't think so.

"I don't think you were blackmailed into it. I don't think you were lured in through a lover. I think you sought it, and I'm asking you to be honest with me, this one time."

I lean back and she looks at me for a long time.

"Honest? You want me to be honest with you?"

"Yes, I do. I realize you have nothing to gain by talking about it, but maybe there's something you want. Something you need that I can do. Just between you and me. A quid pro quo between the two of us. Or maybe you can do it because I'm not the enemy. I'm just a gatherer of information."

"Maybe it's just me," she says, "but doesn't honesty go both ways in an exchange? We both know you're not a psychiatrist. I'm sure of it. Who are you and why do they have you coming here?"

She's not angry as she says it, but it feels like she wants to have a conversation, too, and that's all I need.

I take a minute. And then I say quietly, "I have a wealthy friend whose daughter was trafficked by you twenty-five years ago. He has pulled out all the stops to find her for all these years. A few years ago, they found you and have been trying to find her through you. Then you were picked up.

"He saw it as a way in and hired more ex-CIA and FBI, and he asked me to pretend to be you and go over there, meet with your contact, and see if we could find her. So, it's not some agent going in, it's me, a friend of a father whose daughter's life was ruined the minute you saw her.

"I'm a photographer with zero experience in all this. I'm way out of my comfort zone, but he trusts me. To *be* you, they thought I should meet you. That's it."

I can see surprise on her face. Whatever she had fantasized about who I was and what I was doing, this was not it. She looks relieved almost.

I go on. "If they find out I told you this, the entire operation, which is moving along, will be tanked. I don't want that. I want to do what I'm doing. I'm terrified sometimes, but I want to do it. And I've taken a great risk telling you all this. I'm trusting you. Now it's your turn."

Ava holds up her hand. "Wait. Is this how I got caught?"

"No, it was the FBI."

She looks around. "Is the FBI working with you? How do you know it's safe in here? That no one is watching. I've never believed we are in here alone."

I take out my sweeper, put it on the table and tell her that I swept the room myself; that this was the first time I have done it. I am confident no one is listening.

I tell her that we have on our payroll major players in the FBI unofficially working with us and that's how we were given access to speak to her. That no one from the government has any idea she and I are speaking.

She sits back and I can tell she's assessing the situation. Deciding what she wants to say next.

"I need you to do something for me. If you say you will, I'll tell you my story."

"What is it?" I ask.

"Say you'll do it first. Then I will tell you."

"What if I say I will and then don't?"

"Don't think I haven't thought of that, but I don't have any other choice. I have to hope you'll do it if you say you will."

I pause and look at my hands for a moment. "Okay, I'll do it."

She is quiet and calm when she starts to speak, but she says it haltingly, carefully. "I have a daughter, Laura. She is twenty-five. I had her a few years after I started doing this. She has no idea what I do. She thinks I work for a rich entrepreneur who pays me well. She even met him, or the actor who played him, for dinner a few times.

"I was picked up weeks ago and she will be losing her mind wondering what happened to me.

She will be devastated. And she will lose access to my money. I need you to contact her and tell her that I was killed in Europe, along with the man I worked for. Whatever story you want, just not the truth.

"I have a Swiss bank account and I need you to get her the money so she'll be taken care of. Go with her to access it. I need you to do this," and as she gets to the end of her dialogue, her pitch is higher and she's speaking faster.

I can only imagine how this must have weighed on her these past weeks. And now that she has a way to fix it, as such, she needs to make it happen.

I think about Michael and my own overriding concern that he would wonder who I was and that his life might have been a lie. And Caroline's desire to make sure her children never know the origin of their parent's relationship. And I realize that Ava, Caroline, and I all have something in common.

"Of course, I will do that." And I mean it.

She is changed. I see her now in a way she wasn't showing before. She tells me the story of her past and I take it in. I'm relieved by it. I tear up as she finishes. I'm sad for the girl who made a choice toward rage, revenge and destruction. It doesn't change the evil she's accountable for perpetuating, but it helps me understand the genesis of it. And I know that's what I needed to understand.

She finishes and we look at each other and I smile somewhat sadly at her for the first time since she started speaking.

"Thank you," is all I can think to say.

"Who is the girl you're looking for?"

"I can't tell you that. I won't tell you that."

"Then you found her, or you would ask me to tell you where she is."

I look at her and say nothing.

She sits for a minute and then she says, "If I had it all to do over again, I wouldn't do what I did. I can't make up for it, but I can do one thing to help those who were sold. There's a small metal box in a bank with everyone's name and where they were delivered. The key is in my apartment, in the guest bathroom's toilet tank under a false bottom. It's just the first name of the girl, last name initial, and the last name of the purchaser. But you will be able to create the full list using it. Do what you want with it."

She gives me the information about her daughter and the Swiss bank account, and the bank where the box is, and when she's finished, I can tell she doesn't want our meeting to end. Neither do I.

I want to give her some peace. Maybe she doesn't deserve it, but we all know forgiveness is not for the person who is being forgiven. Except in this case, for me, maybe it is. Ava has paid with her future and her daughter's for what she has done.

"You know, some other woman might have handled what happened to you differently. I imagine that if I were you, that would be what I would lay awake thinking at night right now. But here's the thing. You can't change what you did, but you sure as hell made it a lot better today with what you gave me.

"I hope you can find some peace knowing that. I'm glad I came today to see you. I'll take care of Laura. I'll make sure she is okay. I feel stronger now with what I'm doing next for our operation. I have respect for you and what you gave me today, and no pity."

She looks again at me awhile before speaking.

"Thank you," is all she says. She looks sad, the kind of sad that permeates so much more than the moment of sadness you're in. Deep-seated sadness. I realize that maybe it's grief, and not sadness. It doesn't matter.

Then she speaks again. "I don't think we will see each other again. I thank you for what you will do for me. Good-bye." She gets up, knocks on the door for the handler and doesn't look back as she walks out of the room. I choose to think she couldn't look back. It would have cost her too much, and she had already given more than she ever thought she would.

The flight back is quiet. Rich walks back, sits down and asks me how it went. I look at him and he is so clear-eyed, so seemingly on my team, so present, I respond without a second thought.

"I think I went to try and figure her out. I keep saying it's for my playing the role of her, but I think it's more than that. I think I just wanted to understand what happened to her to make her who she became. Is it nuts that I like her? Care about her even after the unspeakable things she's done?"

He smiles at me. "I don't think so. I've been around people who belong in the electric chair, or worse, and somehow I can understand how they made the decisions that got them there. I learned long ago that we are not the best thing we've ever done, or the worst thing. But I think it's remarkable that you want to understand her. That you want to figure out more than what's on the surface of what happened over these years of torment for so many women. I admire it."

"She told me her story, Rich. All of it, and I'm not telling anyone. And I told her more than I should have about what's happening. Do you think that's a problem?"

He frowns and looks at the floor in the aisle. "Well, we will find out, won't we? You always want only those who need to know, knowing. So, there is a risk, but don't think about that. Focus on what you need to do when we head out tomorrow. I think it will be fine. I wouldn't tell anyone else what happened." He looks at me and smiles. "Don't let your conversation today get in your head for what happens next."

"I didn't give her names or what we are doing. I just told her I was impersonating her. But I'm worried it might be a mistake. A big one."

"We all make them. Don't worry about it."

He gets up and heads back to the cockpit for landing. He doesn't seem overly concerned, and I let that guide me. I think if he thought I'd put it all at risk, he would say so. And I trust he will tell no one.

I can't help but walk through all I learned today as we descend into Palm Beach's airport. None of it justifies who Ava became. None of it. I know that but it gives me some understanding of who she is. And while it doesn't excuse what she chose to do, it makes it easier for me to live with it.

I decide Rich is right. The minute wheels touch down, I must set it all aside and spend the rest of the time until we leave reviewing my role as we head to Riyadh. We have a woman to rescue. We have something to do for Caroline that is all-important to me. I want so much to get it right for her. I think she has earned this.

Then it hits me. I have nothing to worry about with Ava. Quid pro quo. She needs me to make sure her daughter is taken care of. No way will she give me away. My instincts were right. It buoys me up.

I shut my eyes as we touch ground. Tomorrow is just a few hours away.

CHAPTER THIRTY-EIGHT

You Would Be Who I'd Call

The next day on the plane, heading to speak with Caroline one last time, I think about how Robert is willing to do what Caroline wants. Even though he most likely will never see her again, he will do what she is asking him to do.

I recognize that even though he is considered a selfish man, dedicated to his business, his causes, and his day-to-day routine, he loves. He just loves *his* way, and his way includes executing flawlessly what Caroline is asking us to do. I see that love doesn't always take a traditional pathway.

Robert could lose a lot. If we are exposed. If things go wrong. If we fuck it up and Caroline disappears because we expose her, however unwittingly. It reminds me that with every risk/reward situation the risk/reward ratio varies. And the risk this time? Well, it's life threatening, and I intend to do everything I can to make sure my role is done with certainty, confidence, and complete preparation.

I drift off to sleep somewhere over the Atlantic knowing the next days will be stressful, treacherous, and exciting? Is that a word you can use when so many lives are at stake?

A few hours later, I wake to a hand on my shoulder. Rich sits down next to me and says, "We're going to land in two hours, but I want to know if you need to talk anything through."

"Nope, but if I did, you would be who I'd call." I smile and he gives me the space I need to get ready.

CHAPTER THIRTY-NINE

Sound Mind and Body

I'm waiting for Caroline in the same corner of the cafe where we last met. Was it just over a week ago? She arrives late and when she walks in, she's not in a hurry.

She sits down and orders for us both and then turns to me.

"So? I thought we weren't going to meet again."

The daughter is just like the father. Why waste time with pleasantries about how either of us are?

"I didn't feel comfortable giving you all the details over the phone. I thought we should meet again. I also wanted to let you know I spoke to your father about your concern that he might not

283

leave everyone alone. I wanted to look at you in person and tell you he will not contact you again."

She shows nothing. Not a relaxation of her shoulders. Nothing.

"He will leave Amara alone?"

"Yes, but I am sure he will be watching you all and I can't guarantee that if he thinks things have gone toward a bad outcome that he would stand by and not intervene."

She looks at me more closely.

"Why are you saying that?"

"I am a friend of your father's." I realize she had no way of knowing that. She knows nothing about me.

"A personal friend. That is why he chose me. I have been around him for years and you were always in the background, like he was preoccupied. And although I didn't know the details until recently, I knew something weighed upon him.

"This didn't just happen to you. And while I would absolutely acknowledge your incredible ability to survive and maybe even thrive in this unimaginable situation, I know he suffered, too. I can see it now and this decision was not easy for him.

"Some around him felt you had no idea what you were doing or saying when you asked him to leave things the way they are. Stockholm Syndrome. I told your father I thought you were making this decision out of love for your children. And when I think about it, and your two children, I realize I might have made the same decision you're making. Actually, I hope I would have been selfless enough to make it.

"But regardless of whether you are of sound mind and body, he will do it your way and I just want you to know it was *not* the easy decision for him."

I look at her and she is looking past me, but she looks softer.

"I hadn't thought about that," she says. "Thank you for telling me. It was a long time ago that I lived his life and to be honest, I don't miss it. And, while the man you describe is a stranger to me, I will take your word for it."

She stops and looks in my eyes and I can see she is moved.

"Tell him thank you." She pauses and continues, "And please tell him I drew strength from him in the early years. I did."

"I will." I hesitate for a moment and decide to reach out one last time.

"Caroline, do you want to talk about what happened to you? Can I help by listening?"

She says nothing, looking down at the tablecloth for what seems like minutes. She looks up at me, holds my gaze before answering. "No."

She is not angry when she says it. She says it softly, almost kindly, and then continues. "I was lucky … after I wasn't. What has happened to me is unspeakable. I'm lucky with how I now live. My children mean everything to me and their future is the only future I have. That's all you need to tell him."

I don't say anything. I don't need to. The food comes and this time we eat.

Then we play backgammon and we like playing together. We smile and say things. "You are lucky, you know that, right?" Small things that say we are good. It also serves as a cover as I fill her in on the plan details and what she needs to do to make sure the woman is ready when we come. I give her the date and she says I can leave a change of date at the desk of the cafe if it changes. She will check daily.

She stands up to leave. She holds out her hand and I shake it.

"And thank you, too, for doing this; for my father and for me. I will not forget it."

And she is gone.

CHAPTER FORTY

What Happened to Caroline

She somehow makes it to the car and tells Mikal to drive around for an hour before going home. He won't think it odd. She does that sometimes. She closes the partition between them and has him drive around while she looks out the window; looking out at nothing, and thinking about things outside her life. She doesn't do it often, but sometimes.

But this time she closes the partition and lies down on the back seat, in a fetal position and starts to cry. She hasn't really cried in twenty-something years. Not like this. Not like she did in those early months after they took her. After the drugs wore off. These tears come from deep inside, but she isn't afraid they will overwhelm or change her; make her sad or take her to the depths she had known those first months. She knows these are tears that come from somewhere else, someone else. Not her. Not now.

All those months after they took her, after they broke her, after they did unspeakable things to her in preparation for her accepting what her owner would want from her.

And then she woke up one day. And yes, in a flash, she knew what she was going to do. She knew in that morning moment that her life was over. That everything she knew was over. That no one was going to rescue her. That she couldn't fight her way out of what was going to be done to her. That she could die. She had heard one night after yelling, and unusual sounds down the hall, that one of the girls had hanged herself.

She knew on that morning looking out the window at the sun coming up, that she was done fighting. Fearing. She was done. She was going to control what she could. She was going to do the best she could with her own thoughts. She was going to survive, not with the hope someone would finally come and get her out, or she could escape, but so she could carry herself with the knowledge of her own strength.

Yes, they broke her once, but no one could break her again. No one could take from her anything left that was hers. They could think and do what they wanted, and she became very good at numbing herself while certain things took place inside her body, to her body. But the rest of her? That was hers. No one else's. And whatever her life was going to be, it didn't matter. None of it would matter. He wouldn't matter.

She thought of Habil, and that first night. How she felt nothing; not fear, not hate, just nothing. And, over the months as they started talking, she found herself rising to the challenge of making him want to spend time with her. Sometimes she wondered now, all these years later, if she had somehow planned that if he needed her for more than her body, that it could make her life better. That when she stopped taking the birth control pills and got pregnant, that it would get her out of the wing of the compound where she lived, and into the main part of the house she now lived in and ran like it was her choice to be there.

She thought about her children and how they brought her back to life. That her laugh was now real. That she had hopes and dreams, not for herself, but for them.

But then the fear had become that her father would find her and attempt to "rescue" her. That everything that was hers now to control and keep safe would be taken from her. She wasn't afraid for herself but she was afraid for her children. What would happen to them if they were left behind? What would happen to them if they were taken with her? Either way they would be destroyed, and she would never, ever allow that to happen if she could prevent it.

She was relieved that this 'Ava' had shown up, because now she believed that her father would not do anything to ruin this life she now led. Her father wouldn't destroy her children the way she had been destroyed.

Since realizing he had been looking for her all this time, she knew he had experienced some of the pain she had. The unknown. The fear. Over the years she had read in newspapers about him. And her mother. She knew her mother was dead. She knew he was more successful than when she was his daughter. She had seen a picture once, and he looked older, but not broken. Now she knew he was not unchanged by what had happened to her, to them all.

The tears slow and then stop altogether and she feels calm. Relief. Relief that she can see the rest *of her life as it will now be. That her children are safe. She has kept them safe. All this time. She has cleared the way for the life they can lead. That they have a father who loves them.*

She sits up, moves to the window, wipes her face and puts her burka on to hide herself. She looks out and then pushes the button to tell Mikal, "Please return home."

She feels strong. Proud actually. She is a person she created from nothing. There was nothing left when she arrived here. She has two people she loves who are safe, nurtured, and loved. She sits up straight and tall and likes the woman she can see in the window's reflection as the street passes by.

For one moment, she thinks about what her life might have been like if this hadn't happened to her. This nightmare hadn't been hers to live. She closes her eyes. Pointless to go there, and she is grateful for what she has and who she has become.

Mikal turns the car around and returns her to where she lives.

CHAPTER FORTY-ONE

In My Own Head

Five days later I'm on what I think will be the last flight I ever take into Riyadh. The plane is actually crowded when I get on, which I like. There are four women and six men on the flight and they are already sitting in a group in the back by themselves.

I stop by the cockpit and see Rich and Henry and another man I don't recognize. Rich smiles at me then turns to the man sitting behind him. "Justine, this is Philip. Since I will be at the airport running the Riyadh *Home* operation, he will be taking over my pilot duties. He's going to fly us over so I can rest. I will come back and sit with you after takeoff."

I go into the main cabin and take the seat facing forward, leaving the seat across from me open for Rich. I'm a little surprised Coleman is not on the flight but realize that we're going right into the airport in Riyadh and he is on his way to Dubai. Either way I'm good.

I fasten my seat belt and wonder why I'm so calm. I am calm. Not in that ignoring the obvious disaster about to happen way, but in the way that I feel confident. That whatever happens, I'm good. I left a letter for my son, Michael, with my friends Larry and Randy and told them to hold onto it forevermore and give it to him if anything ever happens to me. They were happy to do so. I think they were touched, actually, by the fact that I entrusted it to them. They also have a copy of my new will. But I don't think I'm not coming back.

Maybe I'm just angry? Anger can override fear. I've always believed that anger and hurt are the same feeling and that when I'm angry at a friend, if I examine it, it's usually hurt. Anger is easier than hurt because you can justify it. You aren't as vulnerable. Someone did you wrong is easier, I think, than someone was thoughtless, or even uncaring and hurt you. But I'm not hurt now. I'm angry.

I move to the seat that looks back at the

people who will be executing this mission with me. I get up and go back and introduce myself to each of them. They look me in the eye, shake my hand, but have no interest in small talk. One says, "It's an honor to meet you ma'am," and I thank him. I go back to my seat and realize that they know what they need to do. They trust each other. I'm the wild card and I hope they know I will do my best to not put them in harm's way, because I know they will do the same.

We take off and Rich comes back five minutes after we hit cruising altitude. "You okay, Justine?"

"Is it weird that I am? I'm not nervous. I'm just pissed."

"You will be nervous and when you are, it's okay. It keeps you sharp. Any questions about the plan since we were with everyone? I can go over it with you again if you want."

"No, I don't think so. It's simple. I think what will be hard for me is that I have a small role to play. Depending on everyone else will be the hard part.

"I sent the email to Tariq and we're all set for me to do the drop-off. He was relieved that the girls are enroute. I think he was concerned, or maybe even suspicious when they weren't delivered on time."

"You'll be fine," Rich assures me. "I'm glad

you're going in for this. And they will be too."
He gestures to the people in the back, who are all
asleep, or resting with their eyes closed. He leans
back, "I'm going to get some sleep if you're good.
Wake me up if you want to talk."

He's out in thirty seconds. God, I wish he
could teach me that. I think it would be funny to
wake him and ask him to teach me going to sleep
on command, but I'm tired myself.

We stop in London, refuel and two more
agents get on board. They walk by us and go to the
back of the plane.

Fourteen hours after leaving Palm Beach,
we're descending into Riyadh where it's 9 p.m. local
time, or 2100 hours in my new vocabulary. All the
window shades are down. Everyone is awake, and
Rich is looking at some papers and talking on the
phone. He hangs up.

"Looks like all is good on the yacht. Only one
other couple with the sheik and his companion, and
a quiet dinner, so hopefully we will be on schedule.
I'm going to keep everyone on the plane until they
launch the Zodiacs, and then we will load the van
and get ready to deliver."

I nod and look away. I'm in my own head
now. Still calm.

CHAPTER FORTY-TWO

While They Were Sleeping

The She-KK *team's yacht moves into an alcove less than a mile from the port of Al Batha. They position themselves as the outermost boat, just far enough away to have some privacy but close enough to blend in with the six or so other yachts moored there for the weekend.*

On the deck are two couples, who aren't couples at all but operatives who will be eliminating the sheik later that night. Additional SEALs are stationed in rooms below deck and will only come out under the cover of darkness.

Four more on deck are dressed as staff; all in khakis and white sports shirts with the boat's name, Sirius, on the chest. They wear boating shoes and

*handle the navigation of the yacht and the service
for the two couples enjoying their afternoon of sun,
lunch and book reading. They all look like everyone
else in the area.*

*Well into the evening, they serve dinner in the
dining room that can be seen by the skiffs carting
other boats' guests to the shore for dinner and a
walk around town. Nothing stands out. All calm.*

*Around 11 p.m. everyone heads below
deck. They change into black assault gear, add
their technology and ear buds, and put together
the bags they will carry on the Zodiac boats that
will leave at midnight to go to the Faliz yacht. If
all goes according to plan, Sheik Faliz will not
see the light of day.*

*They congregate in groups of four, just below
deck, by their assigned boats. At midnight, the first
group emerges on the side of the yacht opposite the
port, where no one in the moonless night can see
them. Their black Zodiac is lowered over the side
of the yacht and as it self-inflates, everyone stands
ready to board in the order they will sit. Helmsman
at the stern. Well-armed leader in the bow. Two
others in the middle.*

*Quiet. No one needs to speak. When all four
Zodiacs are in the water and loaded, the captain,
now in all black, looks at his watch. Three minutes*

per boat. Right on time. It's twelve minutes past midnight and the boats move out silently, in line one-by-one, the mile and a half to the yacht that is already established as "quiet."

As they head out, the team leader alerts Rich on the plane in Riyadh to launch his team. Clockwork.

The sheik's yacht is dark, with only boarding lights visible. No one is speaking in any of the cabins, save one, where the night crewman is chatting on his cell phone to a girlfriend.

According to the skiff that had recently passed by the yacht, there is no one on the bridge and no one on the deck. Security often falls short on boats. They seem like such a safe cocoon against intruders.

It takes eighteen minutes to get to the yacht. They decide to board only on the starboard side as the port side has another yacht too close for comfort.

One boat remains 100 meters out to stand watch, in case they need to deal with any potential intrusions or anyone on the yacht needs assistance.

The three other Zodiacs sidle up to the side of the yacht. With catlike precision and silence, each of the teams climbs on deck, quietly waiting for all the others. One man in each boat stays behind to stand ready for the retreat.

They wait three minutes, and when they are confident that no one has heard them board and no one seems to be around, the back group of three slips into the back lounge at the stern of the boat.

The front team rushes the bow entrance to take over the bridge. Four minutes later, the bridge is secure, and the man who had fallen asleep in the captain's chair, is out for the duration with a syringe sleeping helper.

The third team on the deck enters through the bow and goes to the front stateroom to execute the plan. They assumed when they gathered outside the stateroom, they would have five seconds before anyone would scream. Five seconds to silence the girlfriend, and five seconds to dispatch the sheik.

3. 2. 1. They enter the unlocked stateroom and are on either side of the bed before anyone wakes up. She is injected before she even opens her eyes, but the sheik wakes up before they have him pinned down and pitches forward trying to get to the drawer on the nightstand.

Restraining him, the leader looks him in the eye and quietly says, "This is for the women you'll never abuse again." And he breaks his neck in one quick movement.

Carrying him out of the stateroom, they signal the rest of the team and regroup on the deck, leaving as quietly and quickly as they came. On the way back, they wrap the body in chicken wire, fasten the weights that are on the boat to body and wire, and throw him overboard.

He will never be found.

Thirty minutes later they are back on the Sirius. The captain and first mate emerge on the bridge, turn on the running lights and slip out of the mooring heading toward Abu Dhabi. A member of the team is at the back of the boat changing the name and numbers, and the flag now flying is from the British Isles.

In Abu Dhabi and after that Dubai, they will split up and disembark over a period of two days and disappear into cities across Europe and the United States.

It's noon the next day when the sheik's girlfriend awakens and wanders out of the stateroom to find the sheik for breakfast.

CHAPTER FORTY-THREE

Fingerprint Keypad

We've been waiting in the plane for five hours. I nervously wonder if the people in the airport tower question why we are here. Rich doesn't appear concerned so I mentally repeat his mantra. Worry about your role and trust those around you to take care of theirs.

The text arrives and Rich quietly says, "Load into the van."

We line up to exit the plane in the order we will load the van. Rich surprises me by exiting first and getting in the driver's seat of the van. I exit behind him and walk around to the passenger side, open the door, step into the seat, shut the door and lock it behind me. I look at Rich puzzled and he says, "Change of plan."

I immediately suspect that protecting me has something to do with it.

I notice that Rich is checking the mirrors. We hear the doors at the back of the van close, and he pulls down the visor where there's a screen to check that everyone is in place.

Lining the two sides of the van, the five agents look silently forward. One of the agents is checking for bugs, I think, with a handheld device. Two women (Andra and Erin), and three men (Will, Sean and Tank) who I only met briefly, appear to be mentally reviewing their roles.

Rich puts the van in gear and without turning on the headlights, heads off the tarmac. I notice someone at the gate, who closes it behind us. Rich turns on the lights and heads to the main road.

Based on the trial runs, I know we will reach the compound in fifteen minutes. He drives like it's his daily route to work, and I marvel for a moment at how this is all coming together.

Rich asks me, "You okay?"

"Yes," I answer. And I am. I try not to let the voice in my head start wondering why I'm not nervous. I try to go over my role and realize that I know my role. I know what I need to do. I know that I'm ready to move the checkers and that luck will be with us or not. I get it and will not question anything else.

A few minutes pass and Rich quietly says, "Five minutes."

I reach in the pocket of my jeans and pull out a cell phone. I push auto dial 2 and Tariq picks up immediately. "Where are you? You are late."

I keep my voice calm as I reply, "We're five minutes out. Everything is fine, but it took longer to get them ready. Who is with you?"

Tariq sounds somewhat relieved. "A guard is with me. Everyone is asleep. We are good."

"Okay, see you in a few minutes."

One other person. Let's hope that's true.

We pull up to the gate of the compound and I notice that the outside lights are off. Works for me.

I quietly get out of the van and walk to the back just as Tariq opens the compound door and walks to the gate. Nothing out of sync. He stays on the other side of the gate and I open the doors in the back of the van. Will and Sean, dressed in black jeans and tee shirts, step out and help the two women, dressed in robe-like garments out of the van.

The additional agent, Tank, is right behind the women, who seem to stumble and keep their heads down. I know my guys have guns in their pant legs. I hope there isn't going to be any searching, but if there is, I plan to say it's just a security measure.

Counting me, there are six of us going in, and when we get to the gate, Tariq opens it. His security man who is standing in the doorway, walks down a step, but my guys brush past him as they walk up the steps with the women. Slowly.

We all go into the hallway and it's dimly lit. I know where we are going, or where we hope to go, but I stand there waiting for Tariq to tell me where to go next.

"Follow me." He heads down the hallway to the left of the foyer which is where we thought we would be going. His guy waits for us all to get into the hallway and follows behind. He has a small automatic weapon in his hand.

As we walk down the corridors, I'm stunned by how I know exactly where we are based on our training. It takes a few minutes and we reach a door with a keypad lock on it that requires fingerprint ID. Tariq puts his finger on the lock and the door opens.

Inside the hallway, a woman totally covered with a burka sits on a chair. I think she is our inside person, Daria, and she gets up and walks over to us.

"This way," she says and heads down a hallway with doors on either side. I do not see any cameras in the hallway, but we assume they are there. I walk next to her and Tariq stays in the foyer. Damn. Not what we wanted.

His man is behind the group with me. As we walk down the hallway, Daria looks straight ahead but when we get to a door, she gestures to the right by rubbing her hand across her forehead and I know that is the room where the woman we are extracting, Kamaria, is waiting for us.

Two doors down, Daria stops. She uses her thumbprint to open the door on the right side of the hallway where Andra will be left, and then turns and opens the door directly across on the left side of the hallway, where Erin is to be placed.

I walk into the room on the right side of the hallway and motion to Will to lead in Andra behind me. She is led to the bed, where she sits then lies down heavily, seemingly out of it. Daria walks over to her and says, "I will be back soon to help you. Rest." She turns off the light as we leave the room.

Daria, Will and I walk out the door and as I step through the threshold, I count down to myself, 3-2-1 and in that split second, as practiced, everyone is in motion.

Sean and Tank, who were waiting in the hallway with Erin, disarm Tariq's man in less than a second. Erin pulls out a syringe and he's slumped over in two more seconds. Daria is grabbed and injected by Sean and is down for the count two seconds later.

Tariq's man is moved to the room where Andra was placed, and the camera is disabled. I'm hopeful that Tariq isn't watching, but I have no idea if the security for the compound is paying attention or not.

We move to the door where Kamaria is waiting for us, or we hope she is. Two of the men carry Daria to the door and hold up her limp hand to open the door with her thumb. They move into the room and I'm right behind them.

I walk quickly but calmly to Kamaria who is sitting on the bed. She is huddled under the covers shaking.

"Are you Kamaria?" I ask quietly. "We are here to help you and we haven't much time." She nods her head yes, and we quickly lead her out of the room. Daria is still out cold as she is placed under the covers in the room where Kamaria had been waiting.

It takes us less than 30 seconds to get down

the hallway. I take a deep breath and burst through the door. Our plan is to rush out and have me yell at Tariq something about it being a mess and then head out the door before he has time to gather himself.

But as I open the door, I realize immediately our plan is not going to go as we'd hoped. Tariq is there and he's armed, and there are two other armed men, too. It must have been the cameras.

Everyone is shooting and I feel a bullet hit me and I slump to the ground. Barely lifting my head, I turn to see Rich above me and I say, "Get Daria out."

Then there is blackness.

CHAPTER FORTY-FOUR

Pain and Dreams

I might be dreaming. I'm not sure. I think I'm on the plane and there's a bunch of people around me, and there is Rich and someone is telling him to step back and there is blood and then there is nothing.

And the dreams. I'm back in that room and being searched again. Only this time he doesn't let me get up from the table and he stabs me in the shoulder and the pain is awful, and then I wake up and the pain in my shoulder is awful, and then I'm asleep again.

I wake up a few days later, and I'm in the compound in Palm Beach and I feel groggy and my shoulder hurts like hell, but only when I move a certain way. There is a nurse and I ask her what day it is, and she says I've been asleep for a few days and she will get Mr. Bradbury to come in.

I fall asleep again and when I wake up, she has me sit up, gives me ice chips, and a few minutes later Robert arrives. He looks at her and she leaves. He takes her place, standing by the side of my bed, and says, "Well, you did it. They did it. It's done and Caroline is not exposed, or we don't think she is. And now you are back from the dead."

Then he sits in the chair and pulls it up next to the bed.

"What happened?" I ask.

"What do you remember?"

"I remember being ambushed and then nothing but weird dreams."

"It's been five days. We eliminated them all. Our people went back and got the woman who was helping and extracted her too. We think they will think she is the one who orchestrated it. She has some family somewhere in the United Kingdom and when the time is right, we will make it right with her."

"What about the team?"

"Rich was shot but it was not serious. He was the hero. Got everyone to the plane in minutes.

Even going back for Daria was his idea at the last minute, and it worked."

"I'm tired but I have to tell you something."

"Now? Do you want to wait?"

"No, I want a Diet Coke. Can you get me one?"

He gets up, picks up the phone and it's there. With ice.

"Robert, when I went to see Ava, I told her what we were doing."

He sits back down and stares at me. I can see he's angry.

"I didn't tell her who, but I told her what, and she told me some things. I know where a list of the abducted girls' names is and who they were sold to."

"What? What do you mean?"

I give him the information about where the names are, and then I tell him about Laura and what I need to do. I tell him I want to fly commercially but I want him to arrange it and make sure someone watches over us. I tell him this is what I want.

He sits stunned, and then he says, "Okay, Justine. We will arrange it."

We sit for a few minutes and I start to drift off.

"I'm going to go. But Rich wants to see you. You good with that? I can set it up."

I nod yes and then I'm gone.

CHAPTER FORTY-FIVE

Two Weeks Later

I'm still in the bed in Robert's compound, but I know that I'll be okay. They had to operate on the shoulder, but there will be little if any permanent damage, though jumping jacks are not in my future. I smile when the doctor tells me that and tell him they weren't in my past either.

I know that Caroline is okay too because she sent me a message. To the number I had given her. A text. It came in a few days after we returned.

Thank you. And my dad.

My intuition, bolstered by additional intelligence that's come through, tells me that maybe there are more people involved on her end than I knew about. That what Caroline claimed was her role, when she wasn't sure who she was dealing with, was a lie.

I think she has a whole underground going on to do what she can to protect the taken women and mitigate any additional harm to them.

In her own way she's a hero, at least in my book. I tell Robert this when I see him.

"I'm sorry, Justine, that this happened to you."

"Well, I'm not and I'm okay. And I'm forever changed by this experience and what it brought me and others. I'm grateful you asked me to do it."

He looks relieved. Not that he takes my hand or anything. But I'll take relieved. He smiles.

"Caroline is okay. Amara is okay. You're okay. Thank you."

I remind him that Caroline's use of the word "dad" in her text was the first time she didn't say father. I realize he hadn't seen the nuance of it all, and I tell him that a girl calls someone she likes dad and someone she respects father. It's not a lie.

Over the next two weeks, as I recover, he visits my room for both lunch and dinner every day. We play backgammon and we never speak of any of it again.

Michael comes too and demands to know what happened. I tell him the story that is as close to the truth as it can be. "I got caught in the crossfire of a random shooting, and I called Robert who brought me home and I'm recuperating here."

The day I'm going to go home, Robert comes to say goodbye.

"Robert, I want to go see Ava."

"Why?"

"Because I do. I have something I want to say to her."

Then he tells me. She is dead. Something about a suicide in her cell. I sit looking at him.

"Were you not going to tell me?"

"No, I wasn't."

"Is there anything else you aren't going to tell me?"

"No. But Rich asked again if he could see you."

"Robert, I want to go to Ava's grave. Does she have one?"

He looks at me closely, pulls up a chair and tells me that they staged "her" death after the raid, to make it appear she was killed in the shootout. The only people actually killed were Tariq and his thugs. Rich and I were the only ones injured from our team.

They had a burial for Ava and buried her outside of D.C.

"Why?"

"It was decided that we needed to make sure they didn't come looking for you. And find you."

I sit with that for a minute. Then I tell him that I want to go to the grave.

"I'm not sure."

"Look, I haven't asked for anything. I'm doing it."

CHAPTER FORTY-SIX

Seeing Rich

Five days later, a day before I'm heading back to my house, there's a knock on the door and Rich walks in and comes over to where I'm sitting at a table in a chair next to my bed. He looks tired. But he smiles and I realize how glad I am to see him. Deeply touched that he is here. He looks at the chair on the other side of the table, and I ask him to sit down. I ask him if he's hungry, and he stops for a second, looks at me, smiles a bit shyly and says, "Yes, actually I am."

I laugh and say I am too and ask him what he wants. He says to surprise him and I pick up the phone and ask them to bring us lunch and lemonade. I hang up.

It's awkward, and I'm not sure why.

"Rich, I know you saved me. I heard you threw yourself over my body and that's when you were shot. I also know you don't want me to thank you, but I guess I want to say how happy I am that we are both walking. That we made it. That we got her out. Unless they are lying to me, which is possible, but I know you won't, so I am demanding you tell me what happened after I passed out. I know you will tell me the truth."

He laughs and relaxes and we both lean in a bit. He looks around the room, and then smiles realizing where he is.

"They were not prepared for us. They were no match for our team, but they did get a few rounds off before we took them down. You and I were the only ones hit. Tariq's gun we think. We were all out of there less than two minutes after it started, on the road back to the airport and airborne five minutes after the ten-minute drive to the airport. It couldn't have gone better."

"It's all about minutes with you guys. Makes me think you are paid more by the minute if you use less of them."

He laughs, then looks serious and says, "Well, minutes save lives. The less of them the better."

The salads Niçoise arrive, and we both take a bite.

I look over at him, and I put my hand on the table. He looks at it for just an extra second and then takes it and looks at me.

"Rich, I want you to know you helped me more than anyone. I trusted no one totally except for you. I am so grateful."

He says nothing, lets go of my hand, and says, "Did you know I play backgammon?"

I'm surprised. I hadn't thought that he did anything other than fly and save people and take everything seriously.

"Are you any good?" I ask.

"Are you?"

"I'm getting better."

We lunch and talk while we eat and he asks about Michael, and I realize he is here for more than a "thank you and glad you're okay" conversation. And I know in those few minutes we are eating that he and I will be friends. And, if I'm honest with myself in that moment, I realize I'd like that. More than that.

We play backgammon and we banter a bit while we play. We goad each other.

He is getting ready to leave an hour and a

half later and it occurs to me that there is still a hierarchy between us and I will need to be the one who breaks it.

"Rich, I know you don't do personal, or you sort of alluded to that, but I hope we can see each other. If you want to."

He smiles, pulls out his phone and I give him my number.

We text. Then we speak by phone, sometimes for hours. And, then we meet at my house. Never anywhere else. I still have no idea where he lives. And, then our future begins one night when he finally takes me to him, and we go to the bedroom and it is the easiest, kindest, most thoughtful lovemaking I've ever known. We sleep with him behind me, his arms keeping me safe. And when I wake bolt upright with a dream that is far too real, he is right there, saying not a word but stroking my hair and my back and I fall asleep again. He doesn't mention it afterward, and never does, but I know that the greatest gift of all the gifts becoming Clarice gave me, Rich is the greatest.

CHAPTER FORTY-SEVEN

Where is my mother?

I'm walking with Bay in the woods and I think about Laura. A month after I left Robert's house after recovering from the gunshot wound, I had reached out to her and told her I needed to meet with her about her mother. I flew to New York City and met her at a coffee shop near her apartment on the Upper East Side.

She came in looking anxious and eager at the same time. She appeared to be a well-appointed twenty-something year old. Tall. A little heavyset. She looked around at the crowded room and I motioned her over. She sat down and looked at me without saying anything. I'd mulled over what story to tell; the same one I'd told Michael only she didn't recover? It seemed like the easiest. But then I had the issue about going to Geneva to get the money. How would I explain that?

I looked at her and began. "Hello, Laura. I worked with your mother for years. We worked with a wealthy man who hired ex-CIA to go around the world doing dangerous things. Your mother didn't want you to know what she actually did because she didn't want you to be in danger, and she didn't want you to worry. Your mother loved you and talked about you all the time. We were on a mission around trafficked girls in the Middle East and we were extracting some of them and she was shot and killed. I was shot too, which is why it has taken me so long to reach out to you. Your mom died quickly and didn't suffer.

"In the event that anything happened to her, she had made arrangements for me to take you to Switzerland to get money she placed in an account for you there, or access to it so you could live comfortably."

I paused and added, "I don't know what you knew about your mother's life but she was a good person who had a tough childhood."

She just looked at me the whole time, saying nothing. No tears.

The waiter brought our food. We both just stared at it.

Then she looked me in the eye and spoke. "I know you are lying. I know my mother was damaged and I suspect the story you are giving me is a whitewashed version of what my mother did. I have known, since I was little, that there was something wrong with what she did. The way she was with me told me that. And I knew after a week of not hearing from her that she was most likely dead. I also knew not to report her missing."

She stopped and took a bite of her salad. When she looked back up at me, I saw Ava in her eyes. Tough. Unrelenting. But also deeply sad.

She went on. "Don't tell me the truth. I'm good with your story. Just don't continue with it. Don't say anymore. I'll figure it out, or what I want to figure out. I knew my mother would arrange something like a Swiss bank account for me. She always told me that money was freedom and she always wanted me to be free. It was her life's mission. Please just tell me what you want to do, and what happens next."

I told her, "I have a flight on Monday for the both of us to fly to Switzerland and then come back later that day. If you want to stay you can, but I

will only be with you there for a few hours. I will
be in a disguise. I will not sit with you on the plane
or take the same taxi to the bank. But I will do the
bank transactions with you to make sure everything
goes okay. I will also give you a cell phone number
where you can reach me if you ever need anything,
but only if it is an emergency."

She asked one more question. "Where is my
mother? Where is her body?"

I flashed back to my visit to her mother's grave
at the cemetery. I quickly decided it was safer for
everyone if I didn't tell her about it.

"Her body is gone. She was buried at sea.
I'm sorry."

She left the coffee shop after I'd laid out
the plan, and we made the trip without another
conversation.

I've wondered about her life. I hope she takes
a different road from her mother. I hope she has
peace and friends and laughs often. I hope that
one person who Ava touched was the better for it.
I think this is the only shot at that, and I want to
believe it's possible. I do not Google her to find out
anything. I will never provide a link from me to her.
It's all in the past. Hers and mine.

CHAPTER FORTY-EIGHT

Ava's Story

It's hard to believe it's been over a year. So much has changed. I live in Maine now. When I returned from my trip with Laura, I tried to reclaim my life in West Palm Beach. It took me all of a week to realize I had nothing in common with most of the people I called friends.

I sold my house and found a cottage on the coast of Maine, an hour north of Portland. I go to New York and Palm Beach to see Michael and one or two others I still maintain contact with, but mostly I like being here. By myself.

I like the stark winter everyone said would send me running south. I love the fall here. It's stunning and slow moving. I have a garden.

A small, fenced in space that has butterflies, even though they told me they wouldn't come. I have eagles living next door and I sometimes see them. They are calculating, brutal and magnificent.

Rich and I are together, or as together as two people can be when one of them lives a clandestine life; where each time he leaves, I never know when or if he's coming back.

The last time he was home (Dare I call this home for him? Yes, I do.) he told me he wants to cut back on what he does. I didn't say anything, but I know that what drives him is righting wrongs, and he has given up a lot of his life to do that. Cutting back because he's tired just isn't in his DNA; not the DNA he was born with but the DNA he acquired as he saw what he saw these last thirty years.

I'm grateful for every minute we have together, and I'm so proud of what he does that I don't second guess any of it. I've always believed he might not come back, and that I might not ever know why, and I have come to live with it as best I can.

Bayley knows when he leaves. She senses it and sits in his chair in the living room for a week or so after he's gone. She doesn't lie down and sleep; she sits up straight and looks at the door. I think she's willing him to safety. After a week, she stays away from the chair, and she and I settle back into our own routine.

It somehow works for us. Rich comes when he can and we walk on the rocky shores of Maine, through trails, and amidst pine trees with their perfect posture. We make love, but it's not the core of our connection. We talk about everything, except what he does when we're not together, which is eighty percent of the time. I don't have the slightest need to know where he goes or who he works for; if it's for Robert, or someone else, which I think is most likely the case.

Over the past year I've come to believe that Robert's black ops world was singularly based on his search for Caroline. Either way, what used to be an insatiable need to know the behind-the-scenes story of everything in my path has faded.

Rich keeps me grounded in the fact that for one moment in my life's history, I was a courageous woman. A woman who faced fear, and disapproval and rose to listen to the voice inside, regardless of what those around her thought. My finest hour.

That person is still with me. I doubt that the rush of danger and deceit will be part of my future, but I've stopped trying to second guess what's yet to come. I just know that it's kept alive when Rich looks at me and I see the best version of myself in everything his face registers.

But it's Ava that I think about the most; wish I'd had more time with. I think about the story she told me about why she was who she was. I go over it again and again, with questions I hadn't time to consider that day. I have to be satisfied with it the way she told it to me.

"My mother was an immigrant," she had said. "All she lived for was my future as a successful American. She worked for a wealthy family who lived on Fifth Avenue, and had a daughter, Amanda, my age, who went to the Dalton School.

"As the years went on, we traveled with them, my mother taking care of Amanda and me. Cooking at their house in the Hamptons all summer. Amanda and I were inseparable, although I was always aware of the difference between us and the dependence my mother and I had on her family.

"Eventually I went to Dalton on a full scholarship arranged by her father who sat on the board. We were best friends, but we were different in fundamental ways. She was flighty and didn't care about anything as we got older other than her clothes, boys and gossip. I had the pressure of everything my mother expected, worked toward, to make sure I became somebody. And I took it seriously.

"We graduated our senior year and she was headed to her mom's alma mater, Wellesley. I was headed to Harvard on scholarship.

"Some guys came to her apartment after a post-graduation party, and her parents had already headed to the Hamptons for the weekend. They were drinking. I wasn't. One of the guys came on to me and I pushed him away. The other two guys started to egg him on. Amanda left the room. She just left me there.

"They all raped me. All of them. And long after they left, Amanda came back in as if nothing had happened. I never saw or spoke to her again. When I got home, my mother, anxious about her job and my future, told me it was an hour and to forget about it. It was not an hour. It was the end of my life.

"I went to Harvard, speaking to no one for four years outside of classroom conversations about the schoolwork. I changed my name and rewrote my history, one year after graduating and my mother dying. She died of a weary life filled with angst and fear about never getting her daughter out of the world she was born to. I hated Amanda and all the other girls from her world. I wanted vengeance, and I got it."

I didn't say anything. For a long time. Then I said, "I understand. I'm sorry."

On my walks, I often reflect on her story and how her decision to make rich girls pay ruined her life. Vengeance is never meant to be mine, I think.

I think about Caroline and her daughter. I don't look for them on internet searches because I know better than to tempt that fate, but I make up stories about them in my mind. I sometimes play backgammon on *Backgammon Galaxy* and I occasionally pretend that my anonymous opponent is Caroline.

I haven't seen Robert and I think we are both good with that.

I touch the scar on my shoulder each day and think of Rich and what I was told he did after I was shot. He threw himself on top of me until Tariq and his two accomplices were killed, and then he carried me out to the van himself, staying by my side as they dealt with my wound on the plane and then in Palm Beach.

One of the bullets surely meant for me, hit his arm, so he must have been in terrible pain. I was right. He was the one who had my back. And now he has my peaceful heart.

I spend my free time reading, walking Bay, and I write. I journal. I write letters. I wake up each day grateful for the turn in my life that Robert's mission provided for me. I have no time for the life I led before all of this came to me. I know I live a better life now; that I've never been happier.

And I'm more aware of things that matter, focusing on meaningful experiences rather than simply passing time with people who are treading water, not swimming in it. So, the laps I swim each day now mean more to me than they ever did before.

And Clarice? No, I'm surprised that I haven't watched *The Silence of the Lambs* again. Or I was until I realized I don't have to watch Jodie Foster. I *was* Jodie Foster for a brief moment, and it was wonderful.

Each day I'm so proud of what I did, and how it changed me and gave me the courage to live the life I now live.

During one of our late-night talks, I told Rich about the film and what it did for me. What Clarice Starling did for me. He later showed me a piece that described the flight of a starling as,

"… strong and direct, and they walk and run confidently on the ground, although sometimes they fly erratically in the air."

Me too.

EPILOGUE

Five years later ...

I'm out walking with Bay, and my cell rings.
I look and see that it's Robert. It's been a few years
since we spoke. I think both of us know it could
never be what it was, backgammon and current
events around a table of hangers-on. I had no desire
for that after returning. And to be honest, I felt
safer away from such a public group of people,
when I was supposed to be dead. But I'm not
surprised. I always thought this call might come.

"Hi Robert. You okay?" I ask.

"I'm okay but I need to see you. Can you
meet me?"

"You want me to come to you? I'm not
sure ..."

"No, I'm on the plane. I will be in Portland in an hour, which means if you leave now, you can meet me at the private terminal."

"Okay, I will meet you at the private plane terminal."

We meet for ten minutes on the tarmac. The pilot doesn't even shut down the engines. Robert walks off the plane and stands by the base of the stairs. I walk over to him and we smile at each other for a long moment and say nothing.

"Caroline called the number yesterday. She wants you to meet her at the cafe where you met the last time you saw her. That was it. That's all she said."

I don't say anything for a moment. I will not be rushed, even though he is.

"Robert, I'm supposed to be dead. How is that going to work?"

"It's been five years. You will wear a burka, and we will take precautions to make sure you're okay. She must feel it's safe or she wouldn't make it a public place. I have thought it through. You told me to trust her."

I realize he's not anxious. He knows I will do it. But he's in a hurry.

"Okay, Robert. But I need to leave from here,

and we can connect another way about the details, not in person. I'm not coming to your house."

"Agreed."

As I walk away from the plane, I'm surprised at how calm and clear I feel. Until I know what's going on, I will not overthink any of it.

A few hours later, Rich sends a text that he will be at the airport the next morning at 10 a.m. Coincidence? No way. He's been gone almost a month, and I hoped he would be back soon, but I am always relieved to hear from him. It means he's alive.

So, I will pick him up tomorrow, and then? Well, I don't know. For now, I'm going to go home and make pumpkin bread. Rich loves pumpkin bread. Then Bay and I will walk in the woods.

ACKNOWLEDGEMENTS

It takes a village, and the village at Apricity Publishing watched more time pass than they could have imagined as I wrote this novel. Frances Pearson, who never judges but always cheerleads, and her publishing team, who don't stop until it's perfect—thank you.

To my friend and editor, Carol Rea, who makes my writing so much better than it was when she first read it.

My beta readers: Shanette Barth Cohen, Isaac Betancourt, Daniel Carroll, Joann Cox, Karen Davis, Evie Dworetsky, Marcy Echternacht, Robin Kerenyi, Julee Ketelhut, Robin Miller, Leah Ness, Elisabeth Pearson, Alexandra Peters, Mike Rea, Andrew Singer, Marcelline Thomson, Chris Wasserstein, Allen Weingast, Harriette Weingast, and Larry Wiesler, who authentically critiqued it all with insight, thorough attention to detail, and gentle kindness.

My book club group, who were so affirming that my fear of publishing all but went away. The book club topics at the end of the book are partially due to their input. And to Elisabeth Pearson, without whom Caroline's backstory would never have been told.

Special thanks to ex-Navy SEAL Ozzie for his expert assistance with the operational details. We not only thank you for your service but also for the risks you continue to take to keep us free.

Christine Merser is a visionary writer, podcaster, and columnist known for her innovative approach to storytelling and reflective thinking. A seasoned professional with decades of experience, Christine has built a reputation for crafting compelling narratives that inspire action and foster connection.

Christine's writings showcase her expertise on a wide range of subjects, including politics, justice, and personal growth. Her columns and articles have been featured in *The New York Times*, *Newsweek*, and other mainstream media outlets, while her film reviews have appeared on *Screen Thoughts* and other notable platforms. This is her first foray into fiction.

Christine's work reflects her deep commitment to empowering women, promoting democracy, and celebrating creativity. She writes with a distinctive voice that blends wit, intelligence, and authenticity. Christine's passion for excellence and meaningful connections shines through her extensive portfolio of writings, podcasts, speeches, and more.

www.ChristineMerser.com

I would love to virtually participate in your book club gatherings regarding this book when possible. Input from my readers is invaluable. Contact me at Inquiry@ApricityPublishing.com to check availability.

1. This book is written in first person, present tense, from Justine's point of view. This is rarely done and sometimes frowned upon in literary circles, although some recent novels, *Hunger Games* and *Wild*, for example, are also written this way. Did you notice this difference? Would you have preferred it to be narrated in past tense?

2. The plot is moved along mainly with dialogue (internal and external) and there isn't a lot of description. What are your thoughts on this? Do you prefer more or less description in the books you choose?

3. It's always difficult to write about something as explosive as human trafficking. This is a work of fiction. What do you think about how the topic was handled?

4.   If placed in a similar dangerous situation, would you have said yes to Robert's request to help find his daughter?

5.   We are never in Robert's head. What do you think of him? Good guy or bad guy?

6.   Did Justine like Ava? What is her fascination, or need to connect with her? Is it healthy?

7.   Caroline decides to tell her father to leave her and her children alone. Would you have made the same decision?

8.   What did you think about Justine's relationship with Rich?

9.   There are a lot of references to control in *Flight of the Starling*. Who is in control, self-control, letting go of what you can't control. Has it brought up thoughts about control in your own life?

10. Each of our female characters has strengths and weaknesses. Who do you most relate to? Who do you admire?

11. Backgammon and the strategy behind
    the game mirror some of the strategies
    Justine must employ on her journey.
    Do you play backgammon? If so, will
    you play differently now that you've read
    Flight of the Starling?

12. What is your biggest take-away from
    Flight of the Starling? Is there anything
    you would have changed?

13. I think this would work well as a
    screenplay and would love to walk the red
    carpet. A girl can dream! What actors can
    you envision playing the key roles?